To Tammy,
I hope you enjoy my book.
Keep Rockin
Paul Abraham
2020

THE
GOSPEL
ACCORDING TO
ABRAHAM

FROM DELTA BOY TO
TOUR MANAGER

PAUL ABRAHAM

First edition 2017
Published in the USA by *thewordverve inc.* (**www.thewordverve.com**)

eBook ISBN: 978-0-9989052-9-7
Paperback ISBN: 978-0-9992479-0-7
Hardback ISBN: 978-0-9992479-1-4

Library of Congress Control Number: 2017956050

The Gospel According to Abraham

A Book with Verve by *thewordverve inc.*

*Photo of tour bus on cover courtesy of Rick Fitzpatrick,
who painted the mural on the bus, owned by Jayboy Adams.*

Front Cover Design by Ellen Gray

*Print Book Design by Robin Krauss
www.bookformatters.com*

*eBook formatting by Bob Houston
www.facebook.com/eBookFormatting*

TABLE OF CONTENTS

PART THREE NEW HORIZONS

SCRAPBOOK

PART FOUR HIGHLIGHTS AND LOWLIGHTS

PART FIVE MY TIME WITH BILLY RAY

WHAT PEOPLE ARE SAYING

Ellen Easter Powell,
wife of Lynyrd Skynyrd pianist, Billy Powell

"I love him! Paul was such an integral part of the guys being on the road. A more salt-of-the-earth person, would, I think, be difficult to find. Paul is so fair. He had a lot on his plate looking after these guys! Without a complaint or a whimper he was always, with a smile, doing all that he could do and had people's best interests at heart. They were so fortunate to have Paul."

Randall Hall,
former guitarist for Lynyrd Skynyrd

During my tenure with Lynyrd Skynyrd, Paul Abraham was the calming force, with a smile on his face, when the chaos of touring was tough. We shared many laughs, miles and smiles, and extremely good times like a real brother.

Ed King,
former guitarist for Lynyrd Skynyrd and
co-writer of "Sweet Home Alabama"

Paul is a brother of the road, and I couldn't have done it without his help. And he's SUCH a great story teller!

Iain Monk,
Skynyrd blogger, Edinburgh, Scotland

It is September, 1988 and Lynyrd Skynyrd are about to hit the stage at the Meadowlands Arena in New Jersey. This fresh-faced young Scot, having travelled thousands of miles to see his heroes, makes his move towards the stage. My route is cut off as a large figure looms into view and shoots me a menacing glare. "Move back, son," he orders.

I later found out that it was Paul Abraham uttering those words, delivered with a quiet authority, an assertive tone. It goes without saying that I took a backward step, as if retreating from an advancing Grizzly bear. Over the years, as I continued to criss-cross America and Europe following the band, our paths crossed on numerous occasions. Each time Paul was helpful, gracious with his time and unflappable.

I always imagined Paul not so much as a tour manager—more a high-wire artiste walking a tightrope stretched very high above the ground. A tricky balancing act: on one hand keeping the band happy, on the other, dealing the insatiable demands of the fans who wanted to get close to their idols. Working for Skynyrd, Paul must, at times, have felt as if he was herding cats or juggling rattlesnakes. From where I stood, the Skynyrd fan in love with the band and their music, all I ever saw when Paul Abraham stood before me was a good, kind man. At all times, he exhibited the very best of human characteristics.

Killer Beaz
"world-famous" comedian

Paul Abraham is equal parts psychic, cat herder, gang enforcer, priest, judge-jury-executioner, AND GRIZZLY! With a heart of gold. Love that man. "Save up!"

Michael Peterson
chart-topping musician and songwriter

I have worked with several road managers during my career of 30+ years. I was friendly with all of them, but only became true friends with one. That would be Paul Abraham. He always did a great job handling details, but more importantly, he did a fantastic job taking care of the people he was with. He never failed in that regard. He was and still is one of the finest men I know. What a privilege it has been to work with and known him.

MESSAGE FROM THE EDITOR

This book relates some of Paul Abraham's most compelling memories in his life. Rites of passage, working with celebrities . . . he has many great stories to tell. We hope you will find a connection with Paul and these memories. One thing we've come to learn about Paul as we worked through the details of the manuscript: he is a hard-working, big-hearted man who relishes music and racing and living in the moment, appreciates the opportunities he has enjoyed in his lifetime, and cherishes the impact these relationships have had on his person as a whole.

As is the case with memories and opinions, these are his own. Therefore, any misrepresentation of facts is unintentional and can only be attributed to time and perception.

The book is written in the spirit of sharing experiences and celebrating relationships, for better or for worse, because they created this man, Paul Abraham.

— Janet Fix

FOREWORD

It's crazy of me to think anybody would want to read what I have to say here. I'm just an average guy from a small Mississippi Delta town, and by some strange twists of fate, I have encountered some unimaginable circumstances and met a lot of people, some of them famous, most of them not so. I wouldn't call it being in the right place at the right time. Sometimes maybe being in the wrong place at the wrong time would be more like it. I've experienced all ends of the spectrum in my life. I certainly have had my ups and downs, but thankfully, mostly ups.

I had a wonderful childhood with awesome parents and brothers; although looking back, I wish I had studied a lot harder in school to make them more proud of me. I made fair grades, but I didn't excel, by any means—I got by. And it bled over into my future, I'm sorry to say. It wasn't instilled in me that I needed to *get that degree*, and *get out there in the workforce* and *get that pension*, and *sock some money away . . . What? I need to save money? Well, that's hardly the American way!* I thought a new car was essential for me to "make the scene." Don't get me wrong. I don't regret a single choice. Multiple choices? Yeah. But not a single choice.

My travels have been extensive, from the moment I could drive. I never thought twice about jumping in a vehicle and hitting the open road, and I'm still that way. Riding on a tour bus with a bunch of good ole boys was a perfect occupation for me, if you can call it that. In my twenty-four-plus years riding on those buses and commercial and charter jets, I have been in all fifty states numerous times, and the number of towns and cities would be impossible to count. I've traveled and worked throughout Canada from Halifax to Vancouver, Montreal to Edmonton. I've traveled through France and Great Britain, ridden a ferry across the English Channel, and visited the Eiffel Tower, the Louvre, and the Tower of London. I walked into East Germany under the Brandenburg Gate and literally went back sixty years in time. I've ridden on the Autobahn and also a ferry from Copenhagen, Denmark, to Karlshamn, Sweden. I walked down the cobblestone streets of Amsterdam and had some of the best "coffee" in the world in those shops. I've ridden a streetcar in Tokyo and a bullet train though the Japanese countryside. And to top it off, I have had two vacations, all expenses paid, in Hawaii, and got a paycheck for it, to boot. I could never have won all of this on *Wheel of Fortune*, and I certainly wouldn't have been able to do this kind of traveling otherwise. But again, to be able to do this, always with a group of honest-to-goodness, great friends . . . nothing can top it.

Friends have told me for years that I need to write a book about my life. All of it. Well, here it is in all its glory. The stories included in this book are all true. No names have been changed to protect anybody, although a few may have been left out. Sometimes it might be fun to guess who I'm talking about. I will refer the reader to the following quote by Anne Lamott, a modern-day author:

"You own everything that happened to you. Tell your stories. If people wanted you to write warmly about them, they should've behaved better."

I believe she must have had insight into some of the stories I convey here. No one really expects a rock and roll band to behave, and by the same token, no one should be surprised or offended by stories of a fabled band like Skynyrd. Everybody who has even heard of this band knows they have a storied past. People are screaming out to hear these stories, and I just happen to have witnessed everything I have written about here. It's all factual and exact—to the best of my recollection, at least. Some sad . . . but all true.

Be assured, though, that this book is not about Skynyrd, or Billy Ray Cyrus. It's not about Paul Rodgers or the Bad Co guys. It's about my friends, old and new, my family, my dogs and cats, and some of the people I've worked with through the years. It's about places I've been and people I've met. It's about my life—and the good, the bad, and the ugly facets of it.

This book is dedicated, first and foremost, to my brother Carl. He loved Skynyrd and the music business, and I know he was green with envy when I went to work for them. Rest in Peace, Simple Man. It's for my mom and dad, who instilled in me values that I finally learned to live by. It's for my brother John, who is living his dream and mine in beautiful Colorado. It's for my cousins, nephews, nieces, uncles, aunts, and grandparents who showed me what extended family is all about. It's for my best friend on the planet, Freddie Ravner, the mountain man with whom I spent countless days, weeks, months, and years as neighbor and confidant. And finally, it's for you, the reader, for your entertainment and critique.

I want to pay homage to Billy Powell, Leon Wilkeson, Allen Collins, Ronnie Van Zant, Bob Burns, Lacy and Sister Van Zant, Dean Kilpatrick, Steve Gaines, Cassie Gaines, Big Wally Smith, and Tim Smith . . . all gone, but none will be forgotten. They all touched my life.

Part One

MISSISSIPPI DELTA BOYS

LELAND, MISSISSIPPI

I've always heard it said . . . if you grow up in the Mississippi Delta, a part of your heart will always stay in the Mississippi Delta, no matter where you roam, and you will eventually return. I swore up and down, so many times, I would NEVER go back to the Delta. Well, after thirty-plus years of roaming around the country and the world, I am back, although not to stay, but for the time being . . . back. I've traveled and worked in every state in the union and have choices about where I want to live. I've lived in the Rocky Mountains of Colorado and the hills of Tennessee and just always thought I would return to one or the other, and not the Flatlands of Mississippi. I'm not saying bad things about the Mississippi Delta. It was a wonderful place to grow up. It's just that I had gotten so used to the hills and mountains, and the lack of mosquitos, the Delta just wasn't in my viewfinder.

The past few years in the Delta have been filled with the rekindling of old friendships, making new friends, traveling the rough, old Delta backroads and letting my mind wander back to my childhood and teenage years. The memories are as strong as the smell of freshly plowed Mississippi Delta dirt. So much is still the same.

Highway 61 is still lined from north to south and east to west with fields of long, plowed rows. The tractors no longer use the skills of the driver. The rows are now made using GPS. I guess it just had to be. Crop dusters dot the blue skies in early spring.

I counted at least six planes the other day on the back road from Cleveland to Greenville. Back in the '50s, I recall watching for hours as they made each pass within a few feet of the ground and the flagger, flying in that position for what seemed like miles, occasionally lifting over a power line and then back down. Then the crop duster would swoop up and make that hard bank, and back down for the next pass. These days there are no flaggers, but yes, they use GPS too. When I was a kid in Leland, it was Skeet Edwards and Lloyd Steen; I loved to watch them fly their planes. Nowadays it's Bubba Edwards and David Steen carrying the torch for their fathers. It's a noble and necessary profession in the Delta, and it takes a fearless and maybe just a touch crazy person to be an ag pilot.

Growing up in Leland was as close to a perfect childhood as a kid could want. Everybody knew everybody, and back then, people were still moving in and not out. All my friends and all my brothers' friends were ALL friends. So we had a pretty good support system to keep ourselves content. Little League baseball, touch football, basketball, whatever. We always had enough people to choose a couple of teams and occupy ourselves for many waking hours. The schools and teachers were excellent in Leland, so if you didn't get an education, it was definitely your own fault.

Everything went smoothly in our little town. We had a few Otis Campbells among us, and sometimes, they made the most interesting conversationalists. Like old man Lewellyn, the sign painter—and, boy, was he good, as long as you provided him with some Old Grand-Dad and Barq's Root Beer. He was a soft-spoken, old gentleman who could wax philosophical after he took a long swig from the whiskey and then a short swig from the root beer. After another few belts, he was ready to paint, steady as a rock and freehanded. He lived in an old Airstream out by the Bogue Bridge.

I'm not sure if he had family, but we all befriended him and spent many hours listening to him ramble on while he painted signs. He was always in good spirits, even before Old Grand-Dad. He was genuinely a jolly old man and one interesting character.

Yes, Leland definitely had its share of characters: Italians, Lebanese, Jews, Irish, Chinese, black folks, from every walk of life, all living in perfect harmony in a town of maybe six thousand. We had the Carollos, the Abrahams, the Cefalus, the Morlinos, the Sabbatinis, the Petros, the McGees, the Santuccis, and so many others who came together as a town and created our own little Utopia. Leland was totally self-sufficient from our closest neighbor, Greenville, a town of nearly fifty thousand. Stores like Koury's, Jacobs, Rexall's, Azlin's, the National store, the dime store, Stop and Shop, Abdo's, and Cascio's. All these stores thrived and flourished through all my growing-up years. The Leland Cafe with Papa Joe Zingales, Aunt T, and Miss Josie, serving the best hamburgers and french fries in three states, and helping themselves to the fries from your plate as they brought your order through the kitchen door. Sam's Cafe, on the edge of town, was our hangout after a night of partying. Marie, Sam's waitress, put up with all of us and always threatened to tell our parents we'd been drinking and carousing, but she never did. Kelsey and Melsey Hubbard owned the local poolroom, and we spent countless hours there. Eight Ball and Nine Ball, fifty cents a game. And Melsey would rack each game and stand there waiting for his twenty-five cents. We all led a charmed life and didn't have a clue how good we really had it.

We even have a few famous people who claim Leland as their hometown, loud and proud. Jim Henson, the creator of The Muppets was born in Greenville, Mississippi, in 1936 and lived in Leland until his family moved to University Park, Maryland, in the late 1940s. His character, Kermit the Frog, was named after a member of my church, Kermit Scott, a childhood friend of his.

There is an annual Frog Fest in Leland to celebrate the much-acclaimed life of Jim Henson.

Johnny and Edgar Winter also lived in Leland as kids, where their father, John Dawson Winter, was mayor. The boys were born in Beaumont, Texas, and lived in Leland for a few years before moving back to Texas. Johnny's first album featured the song, "Leland, Mississippi Blues," about being from the Delta.

Johnny and Edgar both became world-renowned musicians and entertainers, enjoying great success. Their musical styles were different as night and day. Some of the old-timers in Leland still remember the two young albino boys that lived on Willeroy Street.

Joe Frank Carollo was born in Leland. He played with Joe Frank and the Knights. Joe Frank and his band played all over the Delta and were quite popular, and along with Tommy Burke and the Counts, had many "Battle of the Bands." Joe Frank left Mississippi and moved to California to pursue a higher status in the music business, eventually forming the band Hamilton, Joe Frank & Reynolds. Their album, *Don't Pull Your Love*, made the top five in 1971 and "Fallin' in Love" hit number one four years later. Danny Hamilton, Joe Frank Carollo, and Tommy Reynolds had previously played in the T-Bones. Their instrumental, "No Matter What Shape (Your Stomach's In)," which was on an Alka-Seltzer jingle first, made it to number three on Billboard's music chart. Joe Frank is still playing music at seventy-five years old in his band called Joe Frank and the World Famous Assistants. And believe me, he's a young seventy-five. He never slows down. His mom and dad in Leland were proud of their son, and we all enjoyed their stories of Joe Frank's success.

Tyrone Davis, the soulful singer who charted with "Can I Change My Mind" and "Turn Back the Hands of Time" was born in Greenville and lived in Leland until he moved to Saginaw, Michigan, and then later, lived in Chicago, which he claimed as his hometown. We all knew differently, but forgave him for his denial. He toured internationally and had a very successful career.

We had no video games, but we did have baseball gloves and bats, and I think one of us had a ball. Some of the older kids in the neighborhood invented a card baseball game that was played with actual baseball cards. Yep, the ones that didn't go in the spokes of bicycle tires were used as the teams on the card baseball field. The game was actually ingenious. I wish I could take credit, but Buddy Petro and the two Inman brothers, Butch and Bob, should take credit.

The right, left, and center field walls were two-by-twelves that we had stolen from Sam Thomas's lumberyard. Behind the wall, there was a space that was stringed about twelves inches wide and ran the entire length of the wall. Baseball cards of entire teams were set up in the individual positions on the field. A marble was the ball, and a ruler was the bat. The opposing pitcher would stand behind the wall and lob the marble to the opposing batter. If the ball hit any card, it was an out. If the marble landed a certain distance from the card, measured by a string on a stick, it would determine whether it was a single, double, or triple. The only way to get a homer was to hit the ball over the fence, and it had to land and stay within the stringed area.

We spent many hours playing this game and collecting the cards. My team was the Milwaukee Braves, and my cards included Eddie Matthews, Del Crandall, Warren Spahn, Hank Aaron, and the entire Braves team. Carl's team was the St. Louis Cardinals, and his cards included Minnie Minoso, Stan Musial, Curt Flood, Bob Gibson, and Ken Boyer. Brother John's favorite team was the Chicago Cubs, and his favorite player and card, hands down, was Ernie Banks. We didn't know what "vintage" or "collectible" meant. At that time, vintage was our grandparents' antiques, not a baseball card that came in a pack of gum. Heck, we didn't have a clue that these cards could be worth a small fortune in years to come. We didn't know we weren't rich or poor anyway. We were living for the day, and that's all that mattered. I try not to think about the collection of cards we had in the '50s and '60s that Mama threw away in the '70s.

Family Dynamics

As young'uns growing up, we always had something to do because we made up things to do. We were expected home, first of all, at five o'clock for supper, and then again when the streetlights came on. We were always there too. We had the utmost respect for my dad, Miller, and his forty-four-inch belt. Thank God for that belt. My mother, Miss Kitty, was one of those "wait 'til your daddy gets home" mamas. Daddy was a good man, but he had a bad temper, leaving very little wiggle room for us boys. If it was something we did to deserve it, there would be no talking him out of the butt whoopin' that was coming.

I honestly think I was the recipient of the majority of his ire. I know Carl could push the limits with him, and John just rolled with the flow. I think I do recall a time or two when he lined all three of us up and disciplined us at the same time. Sometimes Mama had simply had enough of us, I guess.

My dad was a well-respected citizen of Leland, and he knew everybody. He had gone to Leland High just as we had, and played football. His nickname was Babe, and that was what all his old friends called him even fifty years later. I can still hear Charlie and Buster Morlino talking about their old friend, Babe. People around Leland still talk about him and a lot of the wonderful things he accomplished, not the least of which was his recruitment of Dr. John Louwerens to come to Leland, when the town needed a doctor desperately.

◀ Brothers Carl, John, and Paul—
early days.

Brothers Carl, Paul and John—
later days.
▼

My dad became mayor of Leland for a short time. The previous mayor was Perrin Grissom, and he had made a run for the state Senate and won, leaving the mayor's seat vacant. So, Daddy put on a great campaign, and with all the black folks knowing him from his radio station, he was a shoo-in. Once he was elected, along with the daily duties of mayoring, he would get nightly calls from someone saying their cat was up in a tree, or a Leland pothole tore up their car, or almost anything you could imagine. He enjoyed his fill-in term, but opted out of running again. He didn't need the stress. I was enough stress for any parent.

My mother was the absolute sweetest, most caring person on

my planet. Her emotions were carried on her sleeve, and I can guarantee I made her cry way too many times. She was born and raised in a hole in the road in Northeast Mississippi called Dry Creek. Kella Marie Anderson Abraham never wanted anything for herself. She would volunteer in the community, and until she really couldn't do it anymore, she fed the hungry at the Presbyterian Church in Leland. She sang in the Methodist Church Choir and taught Bible study groups. It was always about somebody else's needs, and not hers. People in Leland and Greenville still have wonderful things to say about my mother, even though she's been gone for seven years now. I cherish her memory, and, daily, I regret all the heartache I caused her.

———————

My father had always made sure his sons were exposed to many different activities. We all played Little League baseball and loved the sport. I remember many times Daddy taking us to St. Louis to see the Cardinals play. One time that stands out was when my father asked our neighbor, Buddy Petro, to go with us to see some games over a four- to-five-day span. We went to Detroit to Tiger Stadium to see the Tigers play. They played the Los Angeles Angels, and I remember Norm Cash hitting a home run completely out of the park over the upper deck in right field in a losing effort. A day later, we were at Wrigley Field to watch the 1962 All-Star Game, with players like Yogi Berra, Roger Maris, Eddie Mathews (my favorite player), Ken Boyer (Carl's favorite player), Ernie Banks (John's favorite player), Willie Mays, and Mickey Mantle, among many other famous baseball stars of the era. Years later, I was fortunate enough to meet and befriend The Mick's sons, David and Danny Mantle. They came out to several Lynyrd Skynyrd shows, and they always brought Mickey Mantle-autographed memorabilia.

Daddy also made sure we got exposed to Southeastern Conference football, although just living in the state makes you a fan, and you have to choose sides at a young age. I remember going to many games at Scott Field in Starkville to see Mississippi State play and also to Hemingway Stadium in Oxford to see Ole Miss play.

One particularly memorable game was the Ole Miss/Mississippi State game played in Oxford in 1964. Mississippi State won 20-17. I went on the field after the game, along with a thousand of other kids, looking for chin straps. I had met Tommy Neville, a Bulldog football player, when I was at Mississippi State for band camp the previous summer. I found him on the field and told him "good game" and asked him for his chin strap, which he kindly gave to me. The following year, he was playing for the Boston Patriots.

One other game I recall was the 1980 Mississippi State/Alabama game in Jackson, Mississippi. Mississippi State was ahead 6-3 as Alabama was moving down the field toward the goal line late in the fourth quarter. The Alabama quarterback was hit and fumbled the ball with less than ten seconds on the clock and State won the game. I remember vividly Bear Bryant walking off the field with his head down. He was the greatest coach of all time, and the Bulldogs beat him with their defense that day. That game went down in history for all Mississippi State fans.

We all had bicycles that Daddy bought from Mr. Bowers at the Western Auto. Beautiful bikes, with fenders, tassels on the handlebars, chain guard, lights, horn, and even a rearview mirror. Two days later, it was nothing but a frame, which we thought would make them go faster.

One day Carl was out on Lilac Drive riding his streamlined

new bike, and there was big hump in the road way before speed bumps were conceived. He decided to get a good running start and jump the hump. About the time he cleared the hump, he found out he'd forgot to tighten his front wheel after he'd customized his bike. It came completely off and rolled on down the street, but Carl stopped dead in his track, face-first. I went running down the street, picked him up, and got him back home. It cut him up pretty good and chipped his front tooth. Miraculously, the injuries were mostly scrapes, and they didn't slow him down a bit.

I remember when the new kid on the block, Johnny Spinosa, came by on his shiny new bike with everything intact. We threw rocks at him till he took all his shiny stuff off, and he was then gladly accepted into the neighborhood gang of "bikers."

We traveled many a mile on those bikes . . . Tribbett, Stoneville Woods, Dunlieth, Tate's Indian Mounds, where we defied death by sliding down the tallest and steepest Indian mound on a sheet of corrugated metal. Looking back, it was probably not the smartest thing we did, but by no means, the dumbest. The fact that we all survived our childhood was nothing short of a miracle. In school, my friends and I were known as the Chain of Fools, and we lived up to the title daily.

Growing up in a small town definitely had its benefits, but it also had its drawbacks. If we boys thought we were getting away with things, we were fooling ourselves. Usually our parents knew what we had been doing before we could get back home. We were bad about stealing plums and peaches off the many fruit trees in Leland. We also found Old Man Fratesi's watermelon patch hard to resist. We never took more than we could eat, though. He would threaten us with his shotgun, but he never fired it at us. We were just looking for a thrill.

We would ride our bicycles into the fog of the "mosquito-dope" truck, and later in life, wondered why it didn't kill us, although I'm sure it killed some brain cells. We would dive off the platforms on Lake Ferguson and never hit those phantom underwater pipes everybody said were there. We would have dirt-clod fights, and someone would usually end up in the emergency room getting stitched up. We played tackle football instead of touch, and other than a few broken bones, no one ever got hurt too badly. No concussions that I remember, though now that I think about it, I did see stars a few times.

There was a cemetery for the black folks at the end of Lilac Drive, the street we moved to when I was ten, and I'm sure there were plenty of ghosts and goblins floating around our neighborhood. All the gravestones had pictures of the dearly departed on them, some dating back to the 1800s, but the cemetery was still used when I was a teenager. All the neighborhood hooligans (us) would see the hearse turn off the highway, and we would climb the trees in the cemetery to get a bird's-eye view of the funeral. We weren't being disrespectful. We were simply curious. We found out that most white funerals are somber and the black funerals are celebrations, complete with singing and dancing and a lot of laughing, and unlike white funerals, they would last for hours.

For the record, that's the way I want to go. Don't be shedding tears over me. Oh yeah, and fifteen minutes will do. I don't want to inconvenience anyone.

Musical Beginnings

My love for music was cultivated in elementary school. My two brothers and several cousins joined the high school band. John played drums, Carl played clarinet, and my cousin Mike Smith played the trombone. Cousins Dianne and Jane played in the band as well. My older brother excelled in the percussion section, and when he was a high school senior, he was selected to the USA High School Band and represented our school, state, and country in Nice, France.

I couldn't wait until I was old enough to join the band. I wanted to emulate Cousin Mike. I thought he was the coolest, most laid-back guy ever. He was and is an excellent trombone player, who greatly influenced me, and that was the instrument I wanted to play. He was selected to play in the Lion's All-State Band.

I started playing in the fifth grade along with my cousin, Charles Eddy. He started out on woodwinds and then went to drums. I started and stayed with the trombone. We became members of the high school band in the sixth grade. Charly's music career continues to this day at the Delta Music Institute at Delta State University, where I am an occasional lecturer.

Our band director at Leland High was Ernest Cadden. To quote Dan Fogelberg, "He had a thundering velvet hand," and he had us in his palm. He showed how to exude emotion with an instrument. Our high school band was very, very good. We religiously scored straight superiors at the Mississippi High

School Band contest. We were there with the intention of making Mr. Cadden and all our parents proud.

The trips on the bus to and from Jackson were fun too. We were well chaperoned in those days, but boys and girls would be boys and girls. Our band recorded a live album in the high school auditorium, and I still have a copy of the vinyl. The last time I listened to it, I couldn't believe it was a high school band, much less that I had played in it. I was first-chair trombone from the ninth grade till graduation. I'm proud of the many years I played and only regret that I haven't picked up a trombone since. I've picked up a few guitars, but no trombones. That is sad.

We'll Have You Back in Thirty Minutes!

T he farmers of the Delta were a mighty hardy bunch, going from sunup in the burning Delta sun, to sundown, getting the seed in the ground and praying Mother Nature cooperated with them better than the year before. Most all of the farmers around Leland could be seen at Fratesi's grocery for morning coffee, and then again at lunch, and finally, back at the store for a beer or two back in the evening. It was and still is the hangout, or the East End Country Club and Mall, as it is known in these parts. Back in the day, Tony and Larry Fratesi ran the store and folks like the Pieralisis, the Ruggeris, the Zepponis, and the Palasinis might be found at the store at any time, and today those names still frequent the store. It was a place where, if you would listen, you could learn an awful lot. There was a whole lot of truths spoken in that place and sometimes, although rarely, a lie.

One day, I was at Fratesi's getting gas, and this big ole truck pulled up behind me and laid on his air horn. Scared the hell outta me. I turned around to see someone I liked but stayed the hell away from. He was just plain crazy. A good ole boy, but CRAZY. His name was Leo "Bubba" Gerdes. He said he needed me to ride with him and Peck Phillips to help them load some railroad ties. Before thinking about all the times I'd heard people inside that store say, "NEVER get in the truck with Bubba Gerdes" . . . well,

17

that was no lie, and what did I do? I jumped in the truck, and Peck slid in behind me. So there I was, a decent-sized young man, with no brain, stuck in the middle of two BIG men, with no brains, who had been drinking whiskey probably all day. Big mistake.

Bubba said, "This won't take long, Abraham. We'll have you back in thirty minutes." That WAS a lie.

Next thing I knew, we were on Feather Farms Road heading toward Metcalfe, a nothing of a town, but it did have a black juke joint, and that was exactly where we were going. Well, out in front of the juke joint, there was a big stack of railroad ties. Bubba and Peck headed for the front door of the joint.

I hollered, "Hey, what about these ties?"

"We'll get 'em in a few minutes," Bubba said.

I walked in the front door behind them, and I mean, it was pitch-black at probably three in the afternoon. I could see a neon light or two, so I walked that way. *Bubba is already talking to the owner about the railroad ties*, I'm thinking. The one thing I haven't mentioned was both Bubba and Peck had mean streaks, and they had come there to confront this man about some money he owed Bubba. So here I was, standing all the way inside this place, thinking something was fixing to go down and I needed to ease on out while I could.

The voices started getting louder and madder, and my pace went from a trot to a gallop. I hit that front door and never looked back. I wasn't sure if there was going to be gunplay or not, but I wasn't hanging around to find out. When I left, I went a different way, kinda hoping that Bubba and Peck, if they got out alive, would go the same way they came, but after I thought about it, they were so drunk, how would they know anyway? I got a couple of miles down the road, thinking, *man . . . it's eight more miles back to Leland and another two miles to Fratesi's*. Didn't have a cell phone— ha! Well, in a few minutes, sure enough, there came Bubba in that oversized truck, which he needed to carry his oversized ego. "Come on, Abraham. Get in. I'll take you back to Fratesi's."

I said, "Fool me once, shame on you. Fool me twice, shame on me!"

"Aw, man, don't be like that."

I headed on down the road. *Adios* to Bubba Gerdes and Peck Phillips. Never again.

I would only see Bubba one time again, years later in New Orleans, a city my friends and I had visited many times. Leland was almost three hundred miles from New Orleans, and that's about how far we would have to travel to party without anybody back home hearing about it.

We were walking down Bourbon Street, a bunch of us Leland "boys," hurricanes in hand, having a big ole time. We happened on a group of folks that were being thoroughly entertained by this guy who looked terribly familiar. When I got a closer look, it was Bubba, in all his glory, singing at the top of his lungs, and strumming on his old guitar. People were throwing money at him, which I may have done myself, just to stop him from all his caterwauling, but I opted to back away so he couldn't see me.

Phil Campbell asked me, "Shouldn't we say hi to him?"

I said, "Hell no! If we let him know we're here in New Orleans, nothing good can come of it. I promise."

Bubba's life would eventually be from him by some young girl's mother. That's all I know, so you can write your own story about that. Bubba sure had his good side though. He was a musician of sorts, though Nashville would probably have rejected him. But now that I think of it, with some of the acts that come out of there, Bubba would have been a headliner.

TEENAGE ANTICS

My senior year, our school yearbook says about me: "Stoneville is his second home. . . Mr. President . . . football player . . . lovable pest." All true, especially the last thing. Still am. Stoneville being my second home was true, and for all of you who are thinking that I'm talking about an altered state of mind . . . no! Stoneville is actually a little burg a mile outside of Leland. Stoneville houses state and federal agriculture research stations, a place where a lot of us kids got summer jobs. I worked at the USDA Cotton Ginning Laboratory during several summers and into the ginning season. The back fence of the property bordered the Jimmy Walker house, a place near and dear to my heart. I dated Edie Walker, and her brother Charles was one of my best friends. They were members of a prominent Stoneville family that owned Walker Farms Dairy.

We played tackle football in their cow pastures; we rode horses through the Stoneville Woods; and we stayed on the lake all summer long. We swam in their pool, and later, when Mr. Jimmy got tired of the upkeep of the pool, we *fished* in the pool. He actually put fish in the pool. The next year, he had us out there cleaning it to get ready for summer.

We had a whole crew of Leland folks: John Thomas Greenlee, Phil Campbell, Billy Guy Carpenter, Phil Cefalu, Elliott Branton, and many others who hung together strong. Our Stoneville friends, Allen Edwards and his brothers, Crooked Foot Larry and Peewanker, were always around too. Our summers were blissful. I was going into my senior year at Leland High School, so we wanted to make sure we had a summer to remember.

The Walkers were big landowners in that part of the Delta, and since they knew we were going to do what boys of that age do, they gave us an old house to do it in. It was out near Bogue Baptist Church. We would go out there after school on Friday and spend the entire weekend, drinking beer, riding horses, and swimming in the bogue. And oh by the way, a bogue is a bayou or a small river. Back then, I'm pretty sure there were no gators in the bogue, but nowadays, pretty much any water in the Delta is subject to being gator-infested. We partied hard, but we never ran the streets, and that was the exact reason the grownups approved. We would have giant parties in the big open field in the bend of the bogue, including bands and barbeque. Word got around, and there would be a steady line of cars and trucks turning by the church, a dead giveaway. It usually would break down pretty early in the morning, and we would stumble back to the house and sleep it off.

One such morning, just about daybreak, the front door was pushed open, and we all thought it was the local sheriff. Back then, the drinking age was eighteen, and I'm sure most of us were at least close to that. Unfortunately, that morning, they weren't there to check IDs. It was way worse.

It was Mrs. Dot Rea Walker and her son, George Rea, and they were mad as hell that the other side of the family had allowed us to be here without their approval. We were asked to kindly evacuate the house and to never return. There was always a huge rift between the two sides of the family, and this certainly didn't make anything better. There never was much love lost anyway, but this ended any civility between the two. Mr. Jimmy ran the dairy operation, and George Rea ran the farm, and the twain would never meet, not that they socialized that much anyway.

But . . . we weren't deterred. The next weekend, J.E. Branton, Elliott's dad, told us we could have the house on the other side of the railroad tracks, just down from their house, to party in. We were back in business. We were a harmless bunch in those days, so J.E. knew we wouldn't disappoint him.

Charles Walker was raised with a couple of young black boys, Amiel Stewart and Isiah Moore, Jr., or June Bug as we called him. He first met them at the Stoneville Store and almost every day after that, Charles would buy their lunch. Charles was very generous with the money his mom had sent with him. The Stoneville Store was the meeting place for lots of farmers and people that worked at the Experiment Station. They had the best hamburgers and hotdogs around with Mr. Neal's specialty, Stoneville Punch, a drink he mixed there at the store. I would say it was 100% sugar. Charles was joined at the hip with these young boys, and we all grew to love them too, and let me tell you, they loved us back. June Bug could do a perfect imitation of Mr. Jimmy when he would get on to the boys for one thing or another, usually something to do with the horses.

Mr. Jimmy was a character. Small in stature but a giant in every other regard. He'd look up at the boys and give them his signature sneer, and he kinda talked through his nose. He'd point at all of them and say, "You boys, I done told y'all about riding 'em horses and putting 'em up hot and wet. Now git out there and take care of 'em." He was a stern man and didn't waste a lot of time talking. He meant business. He had six sons and three daughters, and between him and Miss Mary Edith, they did a wonderful job raising their kids. June Bug's little brother, Diddy, would come around and catch and saddle the horses for us, and I would let them ride around Stoneville in the '56 Ford my father had gotten for us boys to kick around in. Of ALL the days, those WERE the days!

I have the fondest memories of those times, I guess because they came to an abrupt halt. On June 11, 1968, Charles and Elliott left Leland in the Walkers' car, heading to Chamberlain Hunt Academy for summer school. As they were driving down Highway 61 just north of Vicksburg, the car left the road and went into the Yazoo cutoff, a man-made body of water. No one was ever certain what exactly happened, because in those days, the forensics were not as advanced as today, but the consensus was that they had died of carbon monoxide poisoning, since there was no water in their lungs.

The irony of this disaster was I had been asked to drive them down there and bring the car back home, but the Walkers made other arrangements. This was a brutal blow for all of us, but much more so for Junior. It almost killed him, and to this day, he can't talk about Charles without choking up. He lives in Syracuse, New York, and we still speak often. He makes an annual journey back to Stoneville to visit his family who still lives in the same house, a stone's throw from the cemetery where Charles and, since that time, so many more members of his family are buried, most dying way too young. At one time, there were six brothers and three sisters—and now, only one brother and two sisters.

The Walkers' house was always a happy place when we were growing up. Miss Mary Edith and Mr. Jimmy loved their nine kids and all the different friends they brought home with them. There was always something going on, and Miss Cora Brooks was always cooking. She was the "help" but so much more than that. She listened to our problems and gave us some of the sagest advice I have ever heard. It was a place that meant so much to me that I think about it often. I drove through Stoneville recently and somehow it still looks the same, and I can still see us playing football or riding horses or just congregating in the Walkers' back yard. Vivid memories of a wonderful time.

TEENAGE LAKE ANTICS

I f we weren't partying on dry land, we were partying on the lake. Lake Ferguson was formed by the Mississippi River when it flooded in 1927. In the '60s, there was a marina and a yacht club on the waterfront. Parking spots for trucks and boat trailers were filled to the brim, and the lake was jam-packed with party barges, rafts, and people. There was no such thing as sheriff's patrol or the Coast Guard on Lake Ferguson back then, and I don't recall any accidents, although I'm sure there were some. We all knew the rules of the lake and abided by them without enforcement, for the most part.

We lived on the lake in the summertime. Carl had a boat that Uncle Will Abraham gave to him. It was small with a 75 HP Mercury, but it was the perfect size for Lake Manocnoc, a lake in Leland behind Lillo's Restaurant. Carl and Ray Bernie Carpenter spent long hours on the lake as Carl was trying to perfect his skill for barefoot skiing. He was small and learned fast, and he got really good at it.

But the boat met a tragic end. It was parked in the back yard and, one day while my mom was burning trash, the fire got away from her and burned the boat completely up. The insurance covered a great down payment for a new boat, an inboard/ outboard with 120 HP, a perfect boat for skiing. A year or so later, Carl befriended Greenville's Erle Newton, and along with Clark Henderson, John Archer, Hank Burdine, Tommy Gibson, and a few others, organized the Greenville Ski Club. Peter Watzek, a rich old fellow, buoyed off the north end of Lake Ferguson, and the club used the area for practice. Mr. Watzek bought the club a kite and built a ski jump. There was also a slalom course for the guys to develop their skills and possibly compete against other ski clubs. I'm not sure if they ever did compete, but on the Fourth of July, the ski club would put on a show—with barefoot skiers, a kite skier, and slalom-course skiers—between the yacht club and the marina.

MY BROTHER CARL

My brother Carl had a natural temper like my father, something I never inherited, and Carl's temper would rear its head at the worst possible times.

We were playing Babe Ruth League baseball in Indianola. Carl was a starter and a hell of a good baseball player, while I was second-string third baseman. Indianola had a pitcher whose last name was Watkins. He was a lefty, and for some reason—mostly my head messing with me—I had trouble hitting against a left-handed pitcher. Carl had been pulled from the game for something he'd said in the batter's box. Coach decided that I would pinch hit for Carl. The first pitch was right down the middle, and I let it go by. "Never swing at the first pitch" was what I had always been taught.

Second pitch was on the outside corner, and I took it. The count: 1-1.

The third pitch almost hit me, and Carl came off that bench, raging, "You better not hit my brother!"

For a minute, I thought he was going to run out on the field and start a brawl, until the coach decided he'd better intervene. There was no locker room, so the coach sent Carl to one of the cars we came in, and demanded he stay there until the game was over.

The count was now 2-1. I took the next pitch, and the count became 2-2. I knew if the next pitch was even close, I had to swing. Watkins took his stretch and looked back at the runner on second base, who was taking a long lead off the bag. Watkins took his foot off the rubber, and I stepped out of the batter's box. I picked up some dirt and rubbed it on my hands, like I had seen the pros do, and then stepped back in the box.

The next pitch was right down the middle, and I took a hefty swing and connected with the ball. It went through the gap between first and second base: a single to the opposite field. The runner on second took off and the third-base coach waved him in. He scored easily, and that day, I was the most unlikely hero on the team.

We won the game, and as we headed back to Leland, we stopped at Labella's cafe and had hamburgers and milkshakes as a victory dinner. I must say, my brother was ecstatic that I drove in the winning run that day, and it was all because of his temper.

To this day, when I meet anyone who says they knew Carl, I ask if I owe them an apology. Most people never witnessed Carl's temper outbursts, but the folks who did . . . well, they got a show. He never lost a friend, though. To this day, I meet people who remember Carl, and they all loved him, and so did I.

———————

We used to go to all the dances at the armory and the skating rink in Greenville. I'm not sure why Carl would always pick the biggest and baddest redneck to start fights with. He had a way of pissing people off. It had a lot to do with how many beers he'd had, but inevitably, we would be in a fight within a few minutes. I think Carl did this just to see if I would take up for him.

The last time it happened, and I mean the *last* time, we were at the skating rink. I was on the dance floor and Carl broke in on a big, burly guy who was obviously dancing with his girlfriend. Carl didn't care. The guy told him to move on, but Carl being Carl tapped him on the shoulder again.

The guy says, "You want some of me?"

Carl said, "No, but my brother does."

And it would be on like Donkey Kong. The whole dance floor would erupt, the owner would make the band stop playing, and we were booted out the front door.

I don't think Carl did any of this stuff maliciously. He was just a little bit mischievous, and that's what kept all of us in trouble. I can say one thing for sure: there was never a dull moment!

"Mary Jane"

Friday nights in Leland, all of us would gather at the Leland Pool Hall and shoot pool, play the nickel pinball machines, and drink Budweiser in gooseneck bottles. In those days, the legal age for drinking beer in Mississippi was eighteen. It wouldn't be long before we got bored of hanging out and decided we wanted to pull "Mary Jane" on somebody. This was a prank we would pull on one of the younger guys, telling him we were gonna take him out to meet this girl that we all "knew," and that he would get to "know" her too. Her mean, old daddy worked the late shift at Greenville Mills, so she would be home alone. It was getting close to the time when her father was leaving, and we jumped in a car and headed to her "house" way out on the other side of the Stoneville Woods.

Our victim that night was Johnny Reese, a little guy who was no bigger than a minute, but acted like he was ten feet tall and bulletproof. He talked a mean game all the way there. We called him Twiggy Tapeworm, and it made him so mad he could kill us. We stopped about two hundred feet down the country road and started walking toward the house. It was springtime, but it was still a little cool, and there had been recent rains and the road ditches were full. We stopped out by the mailbox and told Johnny to go knock on the door and she would let him in, and we would wait on him to get to "know" her.

About the time that Johnny set foot on the porch, the front

door slung open and a big man busted out with a shotgun and yelled, "I've told you sumbitches about coming around here messing with my daughter." As Johnny turned to run and got almost to us, the man fired the shotgun up in the air, and Johnny hit the road ditch full of water. He swam a little ways, got out, and started running again when the second shotgun blast went off . . . and back in the ditch he went. We were all running, too, pretending to be running for our lives. When we all got to the car, poor ole Johnny was soaking wet and he had run completely out of his shoes.

It wasn't until we were back to the pool hall that we realized we were one person short. We had a friend who was on the police force come to the pool hall and start asking a lot of questions about whether we had been out at Mary Jane's house. He said her father called the police department and told them he had shot somebody, and he was still lying next to the ditch, but not dead . . . yet. Well, poor ole Johnny came unglued about then and started crying and saying he was sorry and that he would never go out there again. Or anywhere else chasing a woman. In a few minutes, the friend who was "shot" showed up at the pool hall with Mary Jane's "father," Doug Womack, and Johnny realized it was all a prank. He was ready to kill all of us. We seriously didn't have anything much to do, so this was a prank that we would pull often. Heck, it was either that or snipe hunting, and it was hard to find someone to hold the sack.

There was another time with Johnny Reese when our whole crew was sitting at Sam's Café, a little frame building, painted white, on the outskirts of Leland. After midnight on the weekends, there would be a packed house and some of the scariest-looking people you have ever seen. The weird thing about that was it would be the first and last time we would see them; the next weekend, there would some different scary-looking rednecks in there. The waitress was Marie, and she was a little tongue-tied, so you had to listen real hard to understand her. And of course there was old Sam Giardina, the owner. We all loved Sam and spent at least a couple hours a weekend in there, just hanging out mostly.

Johnny Reese was mad at me for messing with him that night, and he left in a tizzy. We didn't think much about it, so we finished our burgers and got up to pay Marie and leave. When we stepped out the front door, we noticed a cop car across California Avenue, and then we noticed Johnny Reese's car pulled off the road. They had Johnny sitting on the hood of the cop car and were talking with him. We left Sam's and turned down California and stopped and asked if we could take him home. They said no, because they planned to take him to jail for malicious mischief. He had pulled these huge timbers that had been on the side of the road and dragged them to the middle of the road—an attempt to set up a roadblock for me. Now back in those days, it didn't matter that Johnny was knee-walking drunk and attempting to drive a car. He was going to jail for malicious mischief, and all in all, that was a good thing. He paid a fifty-dollar fine, and it was done.

Honky-Tonkin' with the Brothers

It's been said in certain circles that if a white boy could live one Saturday night as a black boy, he would never want to be white again. At least that's what all my black friends used to tell me. I, along with some of my more daring white friends, would seek out black friends to take us with them up into the honky-tonks, specifically the one in Rexburg on this one particular night. Cecil Lamberson, my brother Carl, Ray Bernie Carpenter, Roger Lamberson, Billy Guy Carpenter, and I had all decided that tonight was the night. I was working at Walker Farms Dairy, and one of my coworkers was a big, broad-shouldered black fellow by the name of Monroe. All his black buddies called him Po' Mule, so that's what we called him too. Po' Mule and his buddies agreed to take us in with them and make sure nothing happened while we were there. We all met up outside the honky-tonk, and you could feel the beat of the music from the parking lot. It was probably ten o'clock, so things were just starting to jump. Po' Mule and a couple of his friends led us into the honky-tonk, and not unlike movies you've seen, everything stopped, and everyone was looking right past our escorts . . . at us. This was in the late '60s, a decade filled with racial animus and strife, and here we were, some lily-white punks busting up in a dark, smoky room filled with a whole bunch of black folks. It was tense for a minute, but when everyone saw that Po' Mule was our friend, they were our friends as well.

We drank their beer and whiskey and danced with their women to the wee hours of the morning with no incidents or ill will. One very drunk black fellow asked Cecil for a light for his cigarette, and almost like magic, Cecil produced a lighter from his jeans pocket. It was one of the cheapo kind that had the control lever to turn up the flame if needed. It was also one of the cheapo kind that would blow up in your face at any time. Sometimes the lever would move in the pocket by itself. Well, Cecil stuck the lighter up to the dude's cigarette and flicked the flint, and the damn thing flared up and singed about half of this guy's face hair. Cecil turned and headed out to the door at a fast clip, and the dude was right behind him . . . til he got to Po' Mule.

Po' Mule stopped the guy in his tracks and convinced him it was an accident. All was forgiven, and the partying continued. Nothing else happened until we got ready to leave and a couple of the ladies decided they wanted to go with us white boys. And Po' Mule, for the final time that night, saved our asses. He stopped the ladies and told us to get the hell outta Dodge because he wouldn't be able to protect us anymore that night. We heeded his sage advice and split . . . lickety-split.

That wasn't the first time, nor the last, that we spent time in a honky-tonk with people of color. Matter of fact, even today, I visit a honky-tonk known as Po' Monkey's outside of Merigold, Mississippi. It's on the Blues Trail Registry, and a lot of famous folks have graced this authentic juke joint. There have been documentaries filmed there, and the proprietor, Willie Seaberry, was a genuine showman. He passed away a year ago, but the place still rocks. The last time I was there, some of the local folks brought John Lennon's sister, Julia, in for a visit. No one was ever shot, cut, or even cussed at in any of the tonks we frequented, and that just goes to show that the only racism we Southern boys knew was out on the dirt racetracks, and in that regard, we were all "racists." In my opinion and experiences through the years, the South, and more especially, Mississippi got a bad rap. Sure, there were some bad apples, but more often than not, blacks and whites got along famously.

TWO-A-DAYS

Our summers were always way too short, because if you played football at Leland High School, August fifteenth was the end of the summer. That's when we started two-a-day practices at the hottest and most humid time of the year. I was never fond of practice, but I loved the games. My senior year, our football team went undefeated and won the Delta Valley Conference Championship. Our coach, John Smith, molded us into a "Crimson Tide" machine with no standout players, just a bunch of guys who played very well together. At the end of the season, we were asked to play in a post-season game, meaning we would have to practice a couple more weeks. We opted out. I'm sure there were a lot of other conflicts, but mostly, it had to do with the number of guys who played football and basketball, which was easily seventy-five percent. Basketball, baseball, track, tennis, band, and chorus—all teams excelled in our senior year. Many championships and other accolades were awarded to our fine school in sports, music, and academics.

The National Guard and Me

About the time of the Vietnam War, I joined the National Guard in the summer of 1969, a time in this country when there was plenty of crazy stuff going on to keep us busy. Joining the Guard certainly didn't ensure a person wouldn't be sent overseas. It was during the time of the Civil Rights Movement in America, and there were flare-ups here and there, and we would occasionally be called out for riot control. We also got the call after tornadoes and hurricanes for theft prevention.

It was August 18, 1969, the day after Hurricane Camille performed her devastation on the Gulf Coast, and we were deployed, at a moment's notice, to Biloxi. We were out on patrol in our jeep, and we got the call on the radio for assistance behind an apartment complex. We rounded the corner to the back of the apartments, and there stood Vince Venuti, my lifelong friend, with a locked and loaded M-16 pointed at a black man with a television under his arm. Both of them were a little nervous. We questioned the guy, and he couldn't produce ID, so we called in the local cops. They basically said to take the television and let the guy go. We stayed on the Coast about a week as I recall, and that was about the most exciting thing that happened.

The highways were in shambles, and the sea wall was no longer there. I remember driving down what was left of Highway 90 running along the coast, hitting a bad spot in the road and our two-way radio bounced off the pavement into the other lane of traffic. A deuce and a half, or should I say a big old Army truck, hit it, and it was destroyed. I was lucky it was the radio and not me that bounced out. Hotels and motels were demolished, and most homes along the beach were destroyed. Jefferson Davis's home, Beauvoir, survived Camille's onslaught, just needing small repairs and restoration after flooding. The hurricane inflicted terrible damage from Mobile to Pass Christian. It was a surreal scene to say the least.

One thing that reminds me to this day of the power of a hurricane: we were patrolling near the old Sea Aquarium, a favorite place of mine, and there was a cane pole that had pierced a telephone pole without breaking. It was an amazing sight that I can still see in my mind's eye.

<hr>

The Leland Unit of the 2nd Battalion, 198th Armor Regiment (2-198 AR) of the Mississippi Army National Guard was known as partiers and/or hell-raisers. We lived up to that reputation, especially when we went to Summer Camp at Camp Shelby. It was a two-week crap game. We would camp in the field for four or five days and then spend the rest of the time in barracks. The PX would sell us cheap beer and whiskey, and we would stay hammered for nearly the whole time, during off-hours, of course. My brother Carl was an APC (armored personnel carrier) driver, who flirted with court martial about every other minute. One day, we were all standing in formation with our commanding officer addressing the troops about something or other, and Carl comes sliding around the corner in the tracked vehicle and throws mud all over anybody within a ten-foot range. The CO fell well within that measure, and he got the brunt of the flying mud. He was fit to be tied. The part of his face and neck that could still be seen was blood red. Carl came over and was "dressed down" pretty badly in front of the rest of us, but he could take it. Carl had sure handed it out enough.

One particular time, we were sitting around a campfire in the Den of Sin, as our area was called. Names like Hunter Moorhead, Anthony Morlino, Reed Stovall, and Aubrey Hutchinson, among others, were members in "bad" standing with this group. We never hurt anybody, or at least not until that night when a new guy from the Scout unit wandered in, and some of our guys were well into their liquor. Eddie Martin was the new guy, but someone hung the moniker of War Baby on him because he was born in Trieste, Italy, when his dad was stationed there in the Army.

Well, one thing led to another, and words began to fly between the guys involved. War Baby was wrestled down, and his hands were bound with rope. A very small sapling was bent over and War Baby's tied hands were thrown over the top. No one knew what would happen next. That was supposed to be a joke, but it was no longer funny. The sapling recoiled and pulled War Baby completely off the ground, and as we scrambled to get him down, the rope had already cut into both wrists, and they were bleeding. Needless to say, War Baby was as mad as a sack full of hornets. He went running off toward the quartermaster's tent, intending to check out live ammo for his M16.

It was not a good meeting we had with our CO a little later that night, but we all survived without being court-martialed or killed. Later, War Baby and I worked together at Walker Farms Dairy and became friends. He never forgave the other perpetrators for his injuries, of which he had permanent scars to show, and he always swore revenge. Not sure if he ever got it. I kept a close eye on him, that's for sure.

It may not have been that same Summer Camp, but we were on

the way back to the Delta from Hattiesburg and convoying on Interstate 55 no more than thirty miles per hour. I was driving the gas truck at the rear of the convoy, and I looked ahead five or six vehicles to see what I thought was a duffle bag fall out of a jeep . . . until I saw it roll onto its feet and run alongside the jeep as it came to a stop. When my truck came to a stop, I jumped out to check on what had happened. Butch Palasini and George Stone were trying to change seats as they were driving down the road, and it hadn't worked out too well. Thank God, Butch was an agile running back on the football team in high school. I don't recall him even being injured from that roll. Lucky son of a gun.

⚞⚟

I wasn't so lucky in a similar situation. It was a Sunday morning, and Vic Fava asked me, Red Cook, and Ray Bernie Carpenter to use a jeep to go to Greenville and jump-start his El Camino. Well, we did, but we had to stop for beer first. We found Vic's car and tried to start it to no avail, so we left it and headed back to Leland. About three miles down the road, Ray Bernie was in the passenger seat, Red was driving, and I was in the back.

Ray Bernie pulled up the handbrake, and the jeep almost came to a stop in the middle of the road. Thank God it was Sunday morning and most sane people were in church about that time. I taunted Ray Bernie to do it again, and this time Red said no, turning the wheel ever so lightly to try to stop him from pulling the brake.

The jeep turned completely over in the middle of Highway 82. The passenger seat bucked forward and came down on my left foot and broke a bone. No one else was hurt, and I have no idea why not. An Army jeep with a rag top isn't the safest vehicle anyway.

As we got out, there were cans of Budweiser all around the

jeep. We started kicking them off into the road ditch, and no one was the wiser . . . till now anyway. We told the CO that we had a malfunctioning brake, and it engaged as we were just driving down the road. He believed it or just didn't want to get us all in trouble. The statute of limitations has long since expired. Now this was about as dumb as anything I ever did, and to this day, my left foot reminds me of my ignorance.

———————

During the same time frame I was in the Guard, a crew of my buddies and I went to a North Carolina ski area with the intention of learning to snow ski. The conditions were horrible. The snow was like kernels of hard corn with large swaths of ice patches. We had no idea what we were doing, but refused to take a lesson. Instead of the usual snowplowing to slow down and stop, the only way we knew to stop was grabbing the little pine saplings at the bottom of the slope. Here we were, among all these rich folks with their fine ski clothes on, and we wore our ugly drab-green Army field jackets. Well, after a couple of runs, I twisted my knee, and my ski trip was over and done, except that we were stuck there for several more days.

That week, we had the worst ice storm that had ever hit the South. I was living in Atlanta at the time, and when we could finally leave North Carolina, I headed back to Georgia with Roger Lamberson and Wayne Hargrove. It was an awful trip with four inches of ice on I-85, tons of cars and trucks off in the ditches, and me with a twisted knee. Finally, we were in the Greater Atlanta city limits, but didn't even realize it. The entire city was blacked out.

I was supposed to go back to Mississippi for a weekend Guard meeting, but I called Benny Ray, our chief warrant officer, and told him of the accident on the slopes. He told me to go to a doctor and get an excuse, and everything would be fine. Upon x-raying my knee, the doctor found that I had torn cartilage and stretched ligaments. He sent the results to my Guard unit, and they decided to send the results to the Selective Service people, and a week later, I was classified 4-F and booted out of the Guard. As much as I would like to think it was my bad knee that got me discharged, I have to say it was my prior shenanigans that made the final decision. I really didn't want out, but it was totally out of my hands, and I was given an Honorable Discharge. After my demise, the Guard got a whole heck of a lot harder to get into, and many units were activated to go to Vietnam and Germany and other outposts across the world.

BIRTHPLACE OF THE BLUES

The Mississippi Delta is known as the Birthplace of the Blues with good reason. As the old saying goes, the Delta runs from the lobby of the Peabody Hotel in Memphis to Catfish Row in Vicksburg, and interspersed throughout this huge expanse of fertile farmland are many birthplaces and homes of the bluesmen and women that put this place on the map. There are Blues Markers all through the Delta highways and byways, denoting the various artists' homes and history. Blues guys like Muddy Waters, B.B. King, Jimmy Reed, Albert King, and Ike Turner, among a long list of others, have claimed the Mississippi Delta as their home. There seems to be more and more out-of-state tags and tourists in the Delta. There are also a lot of folks who come through that speak in foreign tongues, in addition to those foreigners north of the Mason Dixon Line.

I remember many an hour sitting on the front porch of James "Son" Thomas in Leland and listening to his versions of classic blues songs as well as songs he made up on the spot. We would go by the moonshiner's first for some "popskull" to make sure Son was happy. He was Leland's favorite, and he graced many backyard barbeques and aristocrat farmers' beautiful homes with his own blues style with songs like "Catfish Blues," "Big Leg Woman," "Devil Blues," and "Bull Cow Blues." Son became an international star, traveling through Europe and playing to sold-out crowds of eager fans.

He played for numerous public television programs in Jackson. I remember one such instance when my friend Johnny Reese and I took Son and Sam Chatmon, another local favorite from Hollandale and founding member of the Mississippi Sheiks, to Jackson so they could perform their songs on public television. The trip down to Jackson was full of stories from the two of them, usually about some woman who had done somebody wrong.

Sam had so much character in his face. He had lived the life of the blues and performed the blues in his own unique style for countless years in countless honky-tonks. I remember laughing at the improbable situations they talked about, although I'm sure every word was true.

On the way back, we gave a young bluesman from Sidon, Mississippi, a ride back from Jackson. With the whiskey flowing and the stories getting better and better, the driver (me) got a little carried away and got us lost somewhere between Sidon and Hollandale, and anyone knowing the Mississippi Delta roads knows that is hard to do. Roads run north and south, east and west, and are pretty easy to navigate with a straighter head.

As we rolled into Leland at about daybreak, it concluded one of most enjoyable nights of my young life. Today, as I search for memorable events in my life, this one stands out as a once-in-a-lifetime opportunity to serve the bluesmen who served us so well. My friend, Billy Johnson, opened the Highway 61 Blues Museum in Leland, and any day of the week, a person can visit it and enjoy Son Thomas's son, Pat, playing Son's old favorites.

One Sunday morning, I was heading toward Leland on Highway 82. I was living in Colorado at the time, and I was on my way to visit with my mama for a little while before I headed back out west. The night before, I had seen Johnny Winter and Muddy Waters at the annual blues festival in Greenville. I wasn't hung over at all, just enjoying a Sunday morning ride in early fall. Sunday mornings, I would turn the radio dial to 1580 on the AM dial, WESY. I remember as a boy going out to the radio station with my father on Sunday morning and listening to the gospel groups. This particular morning, I remember an old preacher saying, "Now remember to go out and buy your friend some flowers while he can still smell them." I took that to mean: *stay in touch with your friends, so the last time you see them isn't in a coffin.* We should all live by that credo.

I drove west on Highway 82 and turned left on old 61, heading toward downtown Leland. It was surreal when I pulled up to the red light in Leland, looked over in the car next to me, and as I live and breathe, there was Johnny Winter being driven by some lady, and they looked to be lost.

I rolled down my window and shouted out to them, "Can I help y'all?"

Johnny said, "I'm looking for Willeroy Street, where I used to live as a boy."

I told him they had just passed it a couple of streets back. I also told him how much I enjoyed his music through the years and that the previous night's gig had been incredible. He thanked me and asked me if I was from Leland. I told him yeah and that, like his father, my father was mayor of the little burg once upon a time.

He laughed and said, "Yep, that was the biggest mistake my father ever made."

I said, "Yep, my dad said the exact same thing."

He thanked me for the help, and I thanked him for "Leland Mississippi Blues" on his first album, and they turned around to continue their search for his old homestead. It was a chance meeting—being at the right place at the right time.

Today, there is a Blues Trail Marker in Leland at the corner of Broad and Third, laying claim to one of Leland's favorite sons, John Dawson Winter III.

Photo Credit: John Keen Photography

My father always provided for his family with several occupations. He sold insurance and automobiles for a time, but my first real memories of his work came when he and some other businessmen opened an Easy Listening radio station called WESY. For those of you who have seen *Oh Brother, Where Art Thou*, the radio station WEZY, where the Soggy Bottom Boys sang into the can and recorded "Man of Constant Sorrow," could have been depicting the station as it sat in the country just outside of Leland—a small, square building with a transmitter tower in the field behind it. This place was where my love for music was born.

A few years into the venture, my dad decided he would like to change the format from easy listening to soul. During this time in the late '50s, racial strife was rearing its ugly head throughout the South, and to make such a change was a little controversial, to say the least. Some of the partners decided they would rather sell their interest in the station than take the chance that my dad proposed, and the rest is history. WESY became the staple radio station for the ever-increasing black population in our part of the Mississippi Delta and success came quickly to the thriving business.

With deejays like Rockin' Eddie Williams, Bobby Little, Jerome Daniels, Bill Jackson and Clyde Pinckney, the listenership grew, and with its growth in the area, the station became a hangout for the black musically inclined, especially on Sunday mornings. Bluesman Bobby Rush was just one of the soon-to-be-successful and world-famous artists who frequented the station. I remember nights when the phone would ring, and my father would say, "There's my fourth son calling for a loan."

A few years ago, I ran into Bobby Rush at a casino in Tunica. He was there, along with B.B. King and Clarence Carter, to perform for Bobby "Blue" Bland's eightieth birthday celebration. After the show, while we were grabbing a bite to eat, Bobby walked into the restaurant. I walked over to him and told him who my father was, and tears came to his eyes as he gave me a big hug.

He said, "Son, if it weren't for your father, my career never would have brought me to this point in my life."

This spoke volumes to me as I realized what an impact my dad had on Bobby and many other soul, gospel, and blues people in the music business. I am grateful for my father's contribution.

———

My father would bring home thousands of 33 and 45 rpm "For Promotion Only" vinyl records from every artist from A to Z. We would spend hours on end in Mama's living room, going through those records and listening to them all. If it was something we didn't like, the record usually became a flying saucer or a target for our .22 rifles. I remember, in particular, Daddy bringing home an album called *Meet the Beatles!* Well, needless to say, this album changed my life forever.

A couple of years later, my father came home with the news that this band from Liverpool, England, was going to do another US tour and would be coming to Memphis. He had an ad rep in Memphis tell him he could get tickets for the Memphis show, which my father purchased for the whopping price of five bucks each. He got at least twenty tickets, all on the twelfth row, floor level. A bunch of our friends came along with us to witness this history-making event. The Beatles, within twenty-five feet of where I was sitting, and all I could hear was an occasional guitar riff or a harmony line like none other and a steady hum of girls

Eighty police provided security for the Beatles show, which was picketed by the KKK. The Commercial Appeal reported a total of 20,128 fans "heard the Liverpudlians bow to Dixie."

Newspaper clipping from my first concert, the Beatles
in Memphis, Tennessee, 1966.
Newspaper, *the Commercial Appeal*

screaming. They sang through the Mid-South Coliseum's very inadequate PA system, and sound from the guitars came strictly from the amps. Nothing was miked and amplified, but I was there as a witness to a life-changing event and remember thinking at that point: *Now this would be a cool business to go into.* Little did I know . . .

My cousin Charles Eddy (Charly, now) and I decided that we wanted to put a little combo together. We gathered Glenn Miller and Andrew Cefalu, along with their guitars and drums, and became known as the Four—a wonderfully creative name, I must say. We were the first band to play on WABG-TV live for a morning show, and we were asked to play several birthday parties in the area, as well as a steady gig at the Leland teen club. For a couple of years, we were a hard-working band that made very little money, but had an extremely large time, to say the least. Life was good, and we were doing what we loved, playing the music of the day and getting the girls. I remember thinking, *Now we have arrived!* Other musicians around our little burg would get together with us, and we would play as often as we could. There was Johnny Keen on the keyboards and Bub Branton on guitar, and perhaps the funniest guy to ever pick up a guitar, Roger "Turk" McKennon. He kept us laughing all the time. Life could never be any better than this.

As a senior in high school, I was elected class president, simply because my fellow classmates thought I would be a good choice since I could probably get a great band for the graduation dance. We hired the Ole Miss Soul Review to play and, as well as I can recall, they were excellent and kept everybody on the dance floor. As was the custom back then, some friends and I had mixed up a batch of Yucca Flats, a concoction of gin, 7 Up, and assorted fruits, so I don't remember much about the night, but I was told it was the best graduation dance ever.

The next year, my best friend and roommate, Bubba Petro, and I went to college at Mississippi State, and for one year, I lived the life of a happy-go-lucky student—with no thought of actually getting a degree. I was there for the party; therefore I wasn't there long. The next year, I went to our local junior college, affectionately known as Moorhead Tech, or Mississippi Delta Junior College. I did a little better, but decided to leave college to work in my father's radio station, selling advertising at $1.50 per sixty-second spot. I'm not sure what radio time goes for today, but at a buck fifty a minute, it takes a lot of spots to feed a family of three growing boys and a mama and daddy who loved to eat. I can say we never went hungry.

My father loved making peanut brittle and passing it out to friends as Christmas gifts. He would spend hours on end in the kitchen, making his kids' favorite dish, kibbeh. It's a Lebanese meatloaf made with ground top sirloin (lamb in the old country), cracked bulgur wheat, ground onion, salt, and pepper. There were a number of Lebanese families in the Delta, and a lot of kibbeh was made, but I would put my father's at the top of the heap. Johnny, Carl, and I were his taste testers. He would call us in the kitchen before he would put it in a baking pan, and we would sample it raw, which, truth be known, is my favorite way to eat it. If it passed the test, he would put half in a casserole dish and garnish it with sautéed pine nuts, and the rest would go in a big bowl. Mama would make stuffed cabbage and grape leaves, and our meals were heavenly. I carry on my father's tradition of making kibbeh, but it only comes out on very special occasions. Every time I make it, I put on about ten pounds, thus the "special occasion" rule is in effect.

PART TWO

LYNYRD . . . WHO?

Growing Up and Moving On

A long came the '70s, and I decided it was time to leave the Delta for a more diverse setting, a place with more to do and see, more of a music scene, the big city, Atlanta, Georgia. I moved there with my old friend Roger Lamberson from Leland, the star running back and teammate at good ole Leland High. Life was so fast, and we jumped right into it. We found construction jobs and worked pretty hard all day and partied at night. We burned the candle at both ends and in the middle.

———

In the early '70s, I spent a lot of time in Florida, not so much for the weather, but for the beautiful girl I met on Fort Myers Beach. My old friend Robert Hargrove and I were walking along the pier, watching old men catch crabs, and way down at the end, we see these two girls walking toward us. Robert said, "I like the brunette," and I said, "I like the blonde." When we got closer to them, I could see it really wouldn't matter. They were both drop-dead gorgeous! Robert, being much bolder than I was, stopped them in the middle of the pier, and that was when I met the love of my life, Julie. We immediately connected with each other, and that started a sweet time in my life, although it would be short-lived.

On one of my trips back down to Florida, she introduced me to her best friend's boyfriend, and we hit it off, big time. Ricky Freeman and his two brothers had a house built all for themselves by his mother, Reedy. She was extremely rich . . . and lenient on her sons. They were a little wild, which at that time in my life, was okay with me.

One day, Ricky's little brother, Burton, asked me if I would like to go to St. Petersburg and have lunch with him. I thought it would be a good time, so I agreed to go. When we ended up at the boathouse down by Tampa Bay, I was a little more reluctant. I have to admit, large bodies of water unsettle me, and the boat was hardly seaworthy, but I went anyway. We took a route across the bay that wasn't too scary, and Burton was a good boater, so we made it to the Bayside Restaurant without incident. On the way back across, Burton took me on a different route that went directly under the Sunshine Skyway Bridge. For anyone who has ever been across this bridge, the roadway arches right in the middle, climbing so that it seems like you're going to leave the pavement. I literally have had nightmares about this bridge, and here I am underneath it and looking up at this behemoth. A few years later, a freighter hit the bridge and the middle section collapsed; thirty-five people died.

So, the trip across Tampa Bay was almost over, and Burton said, "Watch this, Paul!" I looked ahead and saw a huge yacht moving at a very slow speed with its nose sticking way out of the water and coming toward us. Burton gunned the 100 HP outboard motor to full speed. This boat wasn't exactly the heaviest thing on the water that day, but I was the heaviest person in that boat. When he hit the yacht's wake, our boat was immediately airborne, and I was looking at the surface getting farther and farther away, and then as it started getting closer again, the boat dipped to my side and banged onto the water like a ton of lead. I was waiting for the boat to come apart. It bounced twice on my side and then straightened itself up. Burton was white as a ghost, and I was watching my life flash before my eyes. Obviously, we survived that adventure, and I am certain that Burton learned a huge lesson about Newton's theory that day. What goes up must come down! Hard!

I learned a huge lesson that day too. NEVER AGAIN get in a boat or a car or any motorized vehicle with Burton Freeman.

The days I spent in Florida were blissful. I was in love and enjoying new friendships and all was well. But as everything else in life, all good things must end. Julie was a couple of years younger than I was, and although her parents loved me, they did not like the idea of a long-distance romance in her teenage years. I totally understood, but it left a huge hole in my heart.

EARLY EXPERIENCES WITH LYNYRD SKYNYRD

D uring the early '70s in Atlanta, I got "turned on" to a great selection of live music venues and an even greater selection of live city girls. Along with that came a selection of drugs of choice, of which I did my share. I had first smoked weed with a friend in Leland, who will remain nameless, but he lived in a big red-brick house on the corner of California Avenue and Deer Creek Drive. I was probably eighteen then. So a couple years down the road, here I am in Hotlanta experimenting with drugs, and I will qualify this by saying it was strictly experimental. It was not like the buzz-of-the-day thing. Maybe buzz of the week, or the month. Most drugs other than weed did not agree with me, but I did make the most of my buzzes. I remember going to a club called Richard's in Atlanta and seeing Little Feat with the late great Lowell George three nights straight. Bonnie Bramlett was the opener and sang backup for Little Feat.

Then, within weeks of this, I saw a band called Lynyrd Skynyrd at a club on Peachtree called Funocchio's. This band would eventually change my life. I remember feeling something different about this music. The lead singer was barefoot, singing songs about life in the South, and he sang from his heart. Every song touched a note in me and reminded me of myself growing up in the South. As I recall, at least one of the band members had a black eye at the time. Later, I found out that the lead singer ruled with an iron fist.

At that time, I realized what I wanted to do next. I saw all the people there and how much it cost to get in . . . maybe, just maybe this band would draw a crowd in the Delta. I called my brother Carl and asked him what he thought, and he, of course, was game, as he always was. Along with a few friends from Atlanta, we started the wheels rolling by organizing a company called Delta Blues Productions back in Leland, contacting Terry Rhodes from Paragon Agency in Macon, Georgia, and booking Skynyrd for a show on March 7, 1974, in Cleveland, Mississippi, at the Bolivar County Expo Building, a cavernous, dirt-floored "rodeo" arena with bleachers and two bathrooms (small bathrooms).

There was no stage, so we borrowed two flatbed forty-foot trailers from Bill Hemphill, put them side by side, and *voila! Rock and roll!* We had Miss Anna Mae Bullock, ex-wife of Ike Turner, cater the event with her famous Price Rite Barbeque, the best in the Delta. Advance ticket sales did well, so we weren't sweating it the night of the show, knowing we would at least break even. We did way better than breaking even. And we introduced a bunch of Delta folks to some great new music, a conversation piece for years to come.

March 7, 1974

My first meeting with Ronnie Van Zant came that afternoon at sound check. It was easy to talk to Ronnie, and we hit it off immediately. It was like I had known him all my life. Maybe that was because we shared the same birthday. Who knows? But we were definitely kindred spirits.

Our total contract was $3,500, and much to my surprise, Ronnie had instructed his road manager/everything else, Lee Walsh, to give us a reduction in the contract. He said that $3,000 would be fine, considering how well we had taken care of them that day. Totally unheard of in the music business today, I guarantee it. We did provide them with all the requirements on the contract rider, including a lot of Budweiser for the band and some J&B Scott for Ronnie. It wasn't long after that he left the J&B, opting for Chivas Regal instead, but the Budweiser stayed in place.

We had a local favorite act called the Candy Shoestring open the show—Donnie Brown on bass, his brother Jerry Brown on guitar, and Boogie Hobart on the drums. These guys were great and always drew a crowd in the Delta. We all thought Jerry could be the next Jimi Hendrix, or at least the next *white* Hendrix. They did an excellent job warming up the crowd. During the set change, we had Son Thomas go up there with a guitar and mike and sing the blues, while work went on behind him.

The crowd loved Son. Who wouldn't? Ronnie Van Zant was equally enthralled with Son and asked me to introduce them. I was more than happy to oblige.

Then came a four-piece band from Birmingham called WARM. The guitar player Ray Honea was a small man who played a Country Gentleman guitar that was bigger than he was. And the band was not warm; they were hot as fire.

It was time for Skynyrd to hit the stage, and they hit it hard. I only wish I could recall the set list from that show. I know they played for ninety minutes, give or take a few, and the people never knew what hit 'em. This show is still discussed around the supper table in the Delta. It was perfect timing. Skynyrd was just beginning to get airplay in Mississippi, and folks were wondering who this fabulous band was. After that show, the fortunate four to five thousand people who'd witnessed it had no doubt who Lynyrd Skynyrd was and how far that band would go.

After the show, Ronnie informed us that the band wanted to

stay in the area the next day to hang out with us. We took some of the guys to the famous One Block East and had a few Skip and Go Nekkids (a Mississippi Delta concoction) that night.

Lynyrd Skynyrd opened for the Who on their North American tour, and within a few months after that, they began their own famous Torture Tour, staying out for months at a time and playing all over the US and Canada. The legend of Lynyrd Skynyrd had begun.

Life for this great band was on the verge of taking a running start into the fast lane. It was exciting to watch their rise to extreme fame in such a short time. Because of the Who tour, Skynyrd's first record went gold, and they became a much-wanted commodity for the promoters of the world. They continued to work hard and drive themselves to exhaustion, but they were doing what most local bands dream about.

Ronnie had his hands full trying to keep all those guys in line, and when Ronnie was drinking, his hands became fists. He would fight anybody, friend or foe. Gene Odom, Ronnie's lifelong buddy, came out to help try to keep them all in line. Didn't work. Years later, I was hired for much the same reason. Didn't work then either. The surviving members of the band had survived a plane crash, and some thought they were invincible.

In order to keep the production company going, I moved back to the Delta from Atlanta and left my old friend Roger behind. I went off seeking a fortune in the music business, and he left Atlanta for Florida Bible College, later to become a preacher in Great Falls, Montana. The fast life had caught up with him, and he saw the light. He's doing what the good Lord put him on earth to do. I saw Roger again a few years back when he and I were asked to be pallbearers for our old buddy, Vince Venuti.

Delta Blues Productions promoted a couple more shows in Cleveland in the same venue. We brought in blues legend Freddie King with another Sounds of the South band, Mose Jones, as opener. We co-promoted a show in Jackson with Beaver Productions that featured Joe Cocker and Brownsville Station. The shows did marginally well, but nothing could top Skynyrd. We booked Wet Willie, and after they got a look at the venue and the dirt floor, Jimmy Hall, who'd apparently had a bad night, said they would not play. This venue was definitely good enough for Skynyrd, but Wet Willie, who Skynyrd had left in the dust, opted out. This hurt us terribly financially, and we decided not to take any more chances with this business. Smart move. Promotion is not for the faint of heart.

Carl and I and a lot of our friends continued to see Skynyrd as often as possible as they toured around our area. Each time, we were taken in with open arms, thanks mostly to Craig Reed, and we enjoyed what was the beginning of a long friendship with the band and crew. A few months after our first encounter, I got to see Skynyrd again and visit with them in Little Rock, Arkansas, at Barton Coliseum. Charlie Daniels was on the bill that night, and I spent two hours that afternoon hanging out with Charlie and Ronnie, talking about anything from country music and blues to hunting and fishing.

Before CDB's final song stopped ringing in the building, Skynyrd took the stage with "Workin' For MCA," and proceeded to burn it down. High energy from beginning to end.

Ronnie's vocals were just incredible and perfectly clear, every lyric speaking volumes. Gary Rossington with his laidback stage presence and his Gibson guitars singing his unmistakable style; Allen Collins, his long, lanky presence and playing a thousand licks a minute; Ed King, playing his Strat with such soul and feel and the most tasteful solos ever written; Leon Wilkeson, wearing his many hats, and bass playing that was as melodic as it was rock steady. And then there was Billy Powell, and although there have been many Southern rock keyboardists, like Chuck Leavell and Gregg Allman, nobody could touch Billy—a classically trained musician who started out as a roadie, until Ronnie heard him playing piano. It was this addition to the band that made the band who they were, in my opinion. And on drums, Bob Burns, keeping the whole band moving.

When the band reached "Gimme Three Steps" in the set, the audience was in a complete frenzy and stayed that way to the end of "Sweet Home Alabama."

The band left the stage and stayed backstage for about five minutes. When they returned, Ronnie dedicated their last song to Duane Allman, and with the spotlight on Billy Powell, the opening notes of "Free Bird" rang out through the more-than-adequate PA system. The crowd went wild!

And right when Ronnie sang out, "Lord help me. I can't ch-a-ange," a guy with a military haircut ran past Security and came out on the stage . . . buck naked!

Ronnie stood back, not wanting to get too close to this nutcase, looked over at Security, who was stepping onto the stage to come get this guy. Ronnie waved them off, and he made this dude stay out there until the last notes of the song. Needless to say, his "endowment" experienced the shrinkage factor. Poor guy.

As I was walking out the back door of the coliseum, I saw him sitting in a side room with a blanket wrapped around him. Not sure what happened to him after the show, but my bet would be on Ronnie telling the guards to let him go. He had simply been overcome by "Free Bird." It happened to all of us at one time or another.

Not Such a Free Bird

Within a year of our first Skynyrd show, I got involved with what could have been called the wrong crowd, had a big run-in with the law, and ended up spending three years and four months paying for my stupidity. It's not necessary to go into that too deeply here and now.

Suffice it to say, my very first day at Federal Correction Institution Tallahassee, there was a riot and the whole place was locked down. A few weeks later, I saw a man murdered over a radio. I was very fortunate to have been met at Receiving and Discharge by Mr. Luther Harvey. I guess he had seen so many ruthless criminals come through there that he recognized I didn't exactly fit the mold.

He took me across the hall that very minute to meet Mr. Rentz, Mr. Richardson, and Mr. Newman in the Records Office. They asked me if I would like to work for them as the resident office manager. I, of course, accepted their offer right away. Mr. Harvey had told me the guy whose place I would be taking had been selling info on the other residents and they'd had to let him go. This was an excellent job, and I stayed there for the entire time I was at FCI. Mr. Rentz really took a liking to me and would take me out to eat and visit his family on occasion. At night, I lived right upstairs in an area that was known as the Honor Unit. No hardened criminals or troublemakers were allowed there, and it was a pretty laid-back situation. It was not hard time, by any stretch.

Mr. Harvey allowed me to receive packages through R&D as

long as they were from my father. He really went out on a limb for me, and I loved him for it. Once, he and I went to the mailroom to pick up a package. My parents had been to Hawaii and brought back macadamia nuts and pineapples. When I picked up the box, the bottom fell out and a pineapple hit the floor in the mailroom, followed by several cans of smoked oysters, Vienna sausages, and macadamia nuts. The mailroom officer, who was also a very cool guy, saw the mess and laughed out loud. Mr. Harvey grabbed the pineapple and a can of oysters and gave it to him to keep him quiet. It was a story Mr. Harvey always got a kick out of, and he retold it many times. He was just a good old man, and I have thought about him and Mr. Rentz a thousand times over in the forty-two years that have passed. I had been fortunate in a situation that could have turned out a lot different for me.

I played softball on the team that went out and played teams on the "streets." I was quarterback on the flag football team, and I played a lot of hoops, handball, and racquetball. And of course, my dad had gotten a couple of acoustic guitars that he traded for advertising and had one sent to me. Carl gave the other one to Son Thomas.

I taught myself to play, and I've always been able to sing, so I entertained the "savage beasts" a lot too. I stayed very busy and was always doing something after work. I went to college and picked up enough hours to achieve junior status. I still play and sing, but mostly for myself.

—————

Carl came to see me shortly after I got to Tallahassee and brought a note written on Holiday Inn Starkville, MS, stationery by Ronnie Van Zant and signed by some of the band members with a note from each of them. That little slip of paper carried me through some hard times during those dark days. It's worn and barely readable from all the times I took it out, but it meant an awful lot to me in the hard times.

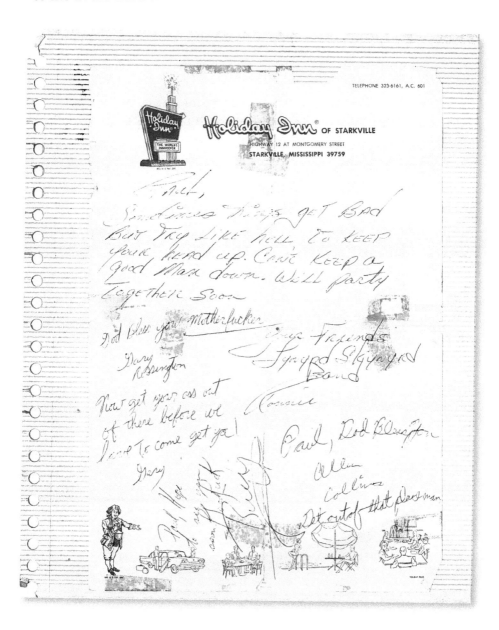

One of my fondest memories while I was "away": I was asked to file a motion for reduction of sentence for a black guy from South Carolina, whose family was going thru terrible hardships. The judge I submitted the motion to came back with a complete reduction of sentence to "time served" and set the young man free.

———————

I hated that I had gotten involved in this fiasco, but all in all, it became a learning experience for me, and I moved on with my life, never looking back and NEVER being that stupid again. I never lost a friend because of it and a ton of old friends came to visit when they could. I saw some horrible things while I was there— things that are still very visible in my mind's eye. I made a lot of friends and had a lot of moral support from the staff and the other "residents." Nothing would ever cure the hurt I'd caused my family, but they, too, forgave my indiscretions, and life went on. That was a long time ago, and although I'm not at all proud of what happened, the fact that it did happen probably saved my life.

HEARTBREAK

October 20, 1977

I was still incarcerated, now in Memphis, getting closer and closer to being released. I was shooting pool with a couple of friends, and we were listening to the radio when a news bulletin interrupted the regular program.

"It has just come across the wires that a plane carrying the Lynyrd Skynyrd band has crashed near McComb, Mississippi, in the area of Gillsburg. There are no reports of injuries at this time. More to come later."

I was devastated. There I was, locked up, and my good friends had been in a plane crash. Totally helpless. I didn't sleep that night, monitoring the radio for any further news on the condition of the band and crew. Nothing! Then as I was getting ready to head out to my work detail in Receiving and Discharge, the word came . . . and not what I wanted to hear.

"Ronnie Van Zant, the lead singer of Lynyrd Skynyrd, was pronounced dead at the scene of a plane crash in South Mississippi. Also killed were Steve and Cassie Gaines, Skynyrd's newest members, and Assistant Road Manager Dean Kilpatrick, along with the two pilots. All other passengers have been transported to McComb Hospital and University Hospital in Jackson, most of them in critical condition."

And there it was. A tragedy of untold proportions, breaking all over the news, and they were talking about my friends. Something in me died that day, along with Ronnie and the others. I was just so thankful that there were survivors.

Leon Wilkeson, Billy Powell, Gary Rossington, and Allen Collins were gravely injured. Artimus Pyle had broken bones in his chest, but had still run through the swamps to a farmhouse for help.

As he walked into the clearing, a farmer named Johnny Mote came out onto his porch to try to find out what had caused the booming noises that had come from the woods around his house. He had his shotgun in his hand, and when he saw Arti, he fired a shot into the air. This did not deter Arti, and he screamed, "Plane crash." Johnny called 911, and although it still took a good long while for help to arrive, the wheels were set in motion.

Lynyrd Skynyrd in front of the cursed plane that crashed and changed the band forever.

Artimus very well could have saved a lot of lives with his actions. He was a Marine, and he let his instincts take over. But his actions could not save Ronnie Van Zant, Steve and Cassie Gaines, Dean Kilpatrick, or the two pilots. That day will long pass, and I will still miss Ronnie, but thank God for his songs.

Carl went to Jackson to University Hospital to check on the injured band members, and he kept me informed of their conditions. He also ran between Jackson and McComb to the hospitals to make sure everybody knew how all the other guys and girls were doing.

A couple of months later, I talked to Billy Powell on the phone, and he described the entire plane crash, from the time they knew they were going down to hitting the pine forest and finally coming to rest in a swamp. He told me about lying in the mud with his nose almost completely severed, and all his friends splayed around him, some dead or dying. It was a horrific story, and although it hurt me to hear this depiction, I felt it helped Billy to talk about it. People who knew Billy will tell you he was an aviation aficionado. He loved flying even after the plane crash.

People used to ask me if I was ever nervous about flying with Skynyrd after that. The odds of a band or any one person being in two plane crashes are astronomical, so "no" would be the answer, although there were occasions later on that were pretty scary.

PART THREE

NEW HORIZONS

PICKING UP THE PIECES

After my unfortunate incarceration was over and my life was given back to me, I came back to the Delta and was welcomed with open arms by all the good people of Leland and Greenville that I had known my entire life. They knew what had transpired with me had been a severe error in judgment; I was a good son and friend, deserving a chance. Sam and John Provenza told my father they would jump at the opportunity to hire me for work at the Pepsi Cola Distributorship, and that was the plan, but another offer came in that suited me better.

I went to work for the Anheuser Busch distributor in Greenville. The owner, Bo Voorhies, offered me a job as route salesman, which I gladly accepted. I worked long and hard hours with my helper, Benjamin Gardner. Ben was a skinny little black man and may have weighed 110 pounds soaking wet; his common-law wife weighed about 450. He told me he kept a fat woman to keep him warm in the winter.

We drove up into Bolivar County every day for four years to service all the grocery stores and honky-tonks, black, white, and yellow. A sober Ben had a hard time with this job. I remember one particular morning, we drove over the levee to call on the Benoit Outing Club. Ben was carrying seven or eight cases of longneck Budweiser on his dolly, and I hear this godawful crash, with bottles breaking and Ben cursing.

When we finally got the mess cleaned up, it was still about

an hour before the liquor store opened, so I pulled the truck in front and did not budge until Ben could get him some Night Train Express. All went well after that. It was a great job; I loved meeting people, and I was damn good at it. I won several brewery-sponsored sales contests and spent a week at the A-B Brewery in St. Louis. We learned everything there was to know about brewing beer, selling beer, serving beer, and drinking beer.

It was just before that when I met Sandie, pretty, petite, and soft-spoken (at first). After being around me for a while, she really came out of her shell, which could be good or bad. We hit it off; one thing led to another, and we were married.

We decided to go camping for our honeymoon, and since her brother, Vance, was stationed in Colorado Springs as a jump instructor at the Air Force Academy, we decided to camp in Colorado. We found a campground called Parry Peak just starting up Independence Pass. We looked out the tent opening at the tallest peak in the state, Mount Elbert. We experienced torrential rains and watched as the river kept growing and growing. We were probably lucky we weren't swept away, but about as fast as it came up, it subsided. Colorado weather. You gotta love it.

We stayed for about a week in Colorado and, upon our return to the Delta, we talked about trying to move to Colorado as soon as possible. I got home and made arrangements for a job in Pueblo with the local Bud distributor. Sandie was a legal secretary, and she had no problem finding work anywhere. She went out first, and I tied up loose ends, gathered up Terrie Lynn, Sandie's daughter, and Dusty, our golden retriever, and headed west into the sunset, leaving behind the Mississippi Delta, I thought for good.

COLORADO

Within weeks of having moved, on June 30, 1983, I got a phone call from home, telling me my father had died. I returned home for the funeral. There was standing-room only in the Methodist Church; people of all colors and walks of life, together to pay their respects to one great man. He was well liked and well accomplished. People still talk about him to this day. I am proud to be called his son.

———

My wife and I loved living in Colorado. We started out living in Colorado Springs and, within six months, had moved to a little cabin in Green Mountain Falls, a rustic little village at the foot of Pikes Peak. We'd purchased our golden retriever from my good friend Robert Austin before we moved. She had a great pedigree, and we decided to find a male golden and have a litter of puppies. Dusty was light blond, and Fletcher, the stud, was dark golden. Dusty had fourteen pups, and the owner wanted a female, so we kept the pick of the litter, a dark golden male with huge feet and a perfect personality. We named him Easy Mountain Breeze, in honor of his grandfather, Easy, a beautiful golden that belonged to my friend Phil Cefalu, and the two of them were inseparable. Phil taught Easy so many great tricks. People around Leland would swear Easy could count money. Rest in Peace, Phil and Easy.

We and our dogs had such a great life in Colorado. We lived

on eight acres bordered on three sides by Pike National Forest. When Sandie and I drove up a winding hill to see the house for the first time, we passed a mountain man with scraggly hair and beard. As I always do, I waved to the guy, and he looked dead ahead, never acknowledging us as we passed. I said, "Whoa! This guy might be a neighbor."

Later, I would find out he, Freddie Ravner, was my closest neighbor, and he lived with two old dogs, Boston and Blue. I figured anybody who loved dogs was all right with me. Freddie and I became close friends and remain friends to this day.

Me and my BFF, Freddie Ravner, and his dogs, Boston and Blue.

We would take our dogs for daily hikes over the mountain and down to the network of beaver ponds below. Freddie was originally from Brooklyn, and although he had been in the Rockies for fifteen years or more, he still had that strong Brooklyn accent. He would call me "Pauly" and usually it was preceded by a "Yo," sounding like someone out of a Godfather movie. Freddie and I shared so much through the years. I still consider him one of my dearest friends, and I miss him every day, but I do stay in touch and see him as often as possible. Whenever one of our tours was coming home from the West Coast, I would always route our travel back through Colorado, so I could go visit Freddie.

One time I went to Freddie's house and he wasn't home, so I sat on his porch and waited for him to come back. I figured he would be back shortly, and while I waited, I enjoyed the peace and absolute solitude of his ten-acre property, complete with an aspen grove, big rock outcroppings, and a stream. His driveway is probably a mile-long gravel road, and I saw him coming as he turned onto it.

He stuck his head out the window of his truck, trying to figure out who was on his property. When he saw it was me, he jumped out of his car while it was still rolling and gave me a big hug. He backed off, showed me a lump on his chest, and told me he had a pacemaker put in a few months earlier.

Later that day, as we were sitting by his stream with his two new dogs, Bear and Bonnie, he had an episode where his heart must have lagged or skipped a beat, but the pacemaker did its job. Scared the crap outta me, though.

Now, keep in mind Freddie's appearance—a true mountain man. We would play one-on-one basketball in my front yard. It was great exercise and a getaway from our wood-gathering chores. I found out that the LA Lakers were coming to Denver to play the Nuggets, so I got us two tickets. You've never seen so many strange looks that were given to us as we walked into McNichols Sports Arena. But we sure enjoyed the game. Magic Johnson, James Worthy, and Kareem Abdul-Jabbar were the stars of the day. I can't remember the score or who had even won, but as a whole, I think Freddie and I were the winners that night.

I am a winner for just knowing Freddie. Despite his appearance—though, admittedly, at the time, I was probably pretty shaggy myself—he is a soft-hearted, kind, and gentle man. He loves animals, especially dogs, but when he lost Boston first and then Blue, he was so heartbroken he told me he didn't want to get any more dogs.

I encouraged him to think about saving a couple of dogs from the pound and giving them this doggie utopian place to live. I urged him not to wait. He called me a few weeks later to tell me he went to the shelter and adopted two black dogs that looked to be part Lab. These were Bear and Bonnie. He took them home and gave them a wonderful life. Freddie is a loner, and dogs are his perfect companions. He talks to them in full sentences, and I'm sure they know what he says.

Another great friend of mine in Colorado was a black gentleman named Larry West. I honestly don't remember how we met, but I'm sure it had something to do with our dogs. He raised imported German shepherds, and I raised golden retrievers. He was originally from Columbus, Ohio, an awesome person and a great family man. His kids called me Uncle Paul.

We spent many hours together in conversation, and we loved to fish together, so when I told him about this hidden lake out in the mountains near my house, he was right there. We drove out into Pike National Forest on rough, old logging and mining roads until we got to a rickety fence and parked. No one for miles around. We saw a bull elk as we climbed over the broken-down fence, and he scampered off at the sight of us. We hiked on down the slope to the small lake and proceeded to catch twelve-inch rainbow trout, one after the other. We were in fishermen's heaven . . . that is, until we noticed the truck coming around the bend of a road on the other side of the lake.

The driver jumped out with a shotgun and yelled at us to get off his property. He was a few hundred yards away, so we grabbed our stringer and headed up the hill, figuring if he shot at us, it would fall short. We went back to my house and cleaned the fish and had a wonderful meal, one of many. We really felt we were innocent because the fence was so rickety, but we did find out the lake was on a "dude ranch" and the guy we saw was the caretaker. Lucky for us, the only way he could have caught us would have been to drive twenty or thirty miles to our side of the lake. The last time I got to see Larry before he passed was as my guest at the Lynyrd Skynyrd concert at Red Rocks. Rest in peace, my good friend.

Jim and Christy Johnson lived on a fabulous piece of property in Cascade, Colorado, and Sandie and I visited with them often. They were caretakers of a property owned by a Kansas family that contained three houses and a swimming pool sitting on the side of a mountain. The owners rarely came to their property, so we enjoyed it for them. Jim and Christy were the first ones to talk us into going skiing at Wolf Creek in the San Juans in Southwest Colorado.

Jim and I also went fishing together at Blue Mesa Reservoir over near Gunnison, Colorado. He had a small ski boat that we put in at the west end of the reservoir near the Black Canyon of the Gunnison. We were camping, so we got there in plenty of time to set up the campsite and do a little fishing before it got dark. We tied off to a sunken Douglas fir tree and began catching rainbows like crazy. They were hitting anything we put on the hook. They even hit a bare hook.

It was a great evening of fishing, and when we decided to head back to the campsite, it was completely dark. I sat on the front of the boat with a flashlight, peering into the darkness, looking for the campground sign. As I panned over the shoreline, I saw two big golden eyes, set wide apart, staring back at me, and fifty feet farther down, I spotted the campground sign. When I finally got to sleep that night, it was not without visions of some big predator watching our campsite.

The next morning, we went to a local cafe to have breakfast and noticed several large cougar hides hanging on the walls. At that moment, I realized what I had seen the night before. We decided not to try our luck there again, and we headed back toward Pikes Peak and the safety of our homes. Of course, anywhere in the Rockies is subject to have cougars, so safety is a state of mind. It was a trip to remember. I'm just glad I'm still here to remember it and not some big lion's lunch.

⚊⚊⚊⚊

While we lived in Colorado, Sandie and I took full advantage of the mountains. We learned to ski at Wolf Creek, an out-of-the-way ski area in Southwest Colorado. Once, when skiing at Wolf Creek, it had snowed hard the entire day, and on the way back down the mountain to South Fork, we were following a snowplow—but he was taking the snow and leaving the ice. We were literally going five miles an hour off the mountain, and the car's front-wheel drive lost traction and started heading toward the edge of the road.

Anyone who drives Colorado's highways and byways knows there are very few guardrails. Well, over the edge of this road was a 1,500-foot drop to the Rio Grande River. I was freaking out, and Sandie could probably see the river over the edge from where she was sitting. Our friend, John Moloney had already experienced an off-road experience going toward Cripple Creek, but he had not been as lucky then as he was this day.

The snow the plow had thrown to the edge of the road saved all of us that day. It kicked the car back into the middle of the lane, and we regained traction. We did okay for a few miles, and then it would happen again, and each time, we were saved by the snow. The car was a front-wheel drive Toyota. The next week, I bought a four-wheel drive Nissan, and we never had that problem again.

We spent weekends exploring the mountains of Central Colorado, often just riding west toward the Collegiate Peaks and Independence Pass, a two-lane road that winds up and over the 12,000-foot mountain pass into Aspen. We would ride out by John Denver's Maroon Bells, a majestic valley that opens to the most awesome peaks in the state.

Some weekends, we would travel north into Boulder, and from there, we would take the Boulder Canyon Road into Nederland and follow the Peak to Peak Highway into Estes Park and the entrance to Rocky Mountain National Park. I remember one particular time when we saw a billy, a nanny, and a kid— Rocky Mountain goats, with their long, white coats and friendly faces. I got out of the car and walked back a hundred feet or so to get a good picture of them.

As I was walking back to the car, I heard Sandie say, "Look, Paul!" I turned around to see all three of them following me; they came right up to the car. Dusty and Easy were going crazy in the car, but that didn't scare those goats. All they wanted was a handout, so I found some peanuts to give them. I know this is not what the Fish and Wildlife people tell you to do, but I figured I would never get this close to a mountain goat again.

Boy, was I wrong! I had another encounter with a goat at Mount Rushmore some years later, when Sly Dog (Billy Ray Cyrus's band) and crew visited—I was part of that group. We were walking up to the entrance from the parking lot, and I was pulling up the rear. Everybody walked past him, but when he saw me, he decided to let me know I was getting too close and lowered his head and started scratching his hooves in the dirt. I decided, for the safety of the goat (ha ha), that I would walk around the parking lot and enter from another direction. All's well that ends well.

Later that day, we visited the Crazy Horse Monument a few miles away. It was quite impressive and even more majestic than Rushmore.

Jackson Hole and Gary Rossington

illy Powell informed me that after the Rossington Collins Band had broken up, and Dale Krantz and Gary Rossington got married and moved to Jackson, Wyoming. This was only six hundred miles from where we lived in the Rockies, so Sandie and I drove there to see the sights; I was hoping to find Gary and rekindle our friendship. We traveled through some beautiful countryside on the way to Northwest Wyoming. High peaks and beautiful rivers and streams were more prevalent the closer we got to Jackson.

We drove into the little town and immediately fell in love with it. The town square adorned with elk antler arches at each corner exuded charm, and the shops that surrounded the square were all tourist-friendly . . . and pricy. We had wandered into the most expensive tourist trap in the country.

We spent the first couple of days seeing the sights around the Tetons and Yellowstone, and then I decided to try to call Gary. His phone number was actually in the local phone book, so I rang him up. His wife Dale answered, and I explained who I was; she expressed her excitement to hear from someone with a Southern accent, not to mention an acquaintance of Gary's. She told me he was at the supermarket, and there was only one, so I shouldn't have any trouble finding him.

I walked into the market, and as I headed up an aisle, I spotted Gary. He had put on considerable weight since the last time I'd seen him, but his coal-black hair pulled back in a ponytail was easily recognizable. After I got his attention, it took him about five seconds to remember me. The first question out of his mouth was, "How's your brother Carl?"

We talked for a few minutes, and he invited us over to his house on the other side of the Elk Refuge. He said I should just follow him, since it wasn't that easy to find. We drove eight miles or so and pulled into his driveway. His house was made completely of logs, that I would find out later were imported from Idaho. He had a five-acre mini-farm that had the most fabulous view of the Elk Refuge and the Grand Tetons in the background. Behind his house was the Gros Ventre Range with the most prominent mountain being the Sleeping Indian, which is exactly what it looked like.

I was amazed at his home, inside and out. I had never met Dale, so Gary introduced me, and I introduced Sandie to both of them. They had a gorgeous little girl, Mary, and Dale was pregnant with their second daughter, Annie, at the time. We visited and caught up on what had been happening over the past few years since we had seen each other.

They were so happy to see anybody from the past that they invited us to spend the rest of our vacation with them. We really had a good time. Gary and I went fishing in what he deemed his "honey hole," which was a beautiful spot just north of the Tetons and just south of Yellowstone. I could actually see the brown trout swimming against the current, checking out the baited hook. And that was about all they did—check it out. We didn't catch a thing, but to be in the midst of God's Country was well worth the effort. There were moose wading in the same river we were fishing in. Who needs to catch a fish? Besides, these were "Gold Medal waters," and anything caught had to be released.

The next day, we went with Gary's friend, Brian, in his boat and fished in Jackson Lake, a beautiful body of water nestled against the Tetons. We were there before daybreak, and when the sun came up and hit the Tetons, it was completely breathtaking. We caught four or five Mackinaw, or lake trout, as the locals call them, and had them for supper that night.

We enjoyed each other's company for a few more days, and then Sandie and I headed back home. It wasn't Jackson Hole, but it was a log house situated on eight acres surrounded by Pike National Forest at 9,200 feet above sea level, so it wasn't like we were going back to the ghetto after being on Park Avenue for a few days.

Some of my favorite people in the world played in a Mississippi Delta boogie band called the Tangents. They were probably the most popular band around those parts for a long, long time. Duff Durrough, Fish Michie, Charlie Jacobs, Bob Barbee, and "Groovy" Parker made up the band at that time. I was living in the mountains of Colorado, and I got a call from our mutual friend, Mike Williams (a.k.a. Sipsack) telling me they were coming through, heading to Jackson Hole, and to pack a bag because I was going too.

The Tangents were booked at the Mangy Moose in Teton Village just outside of Jackson. I guess they knew that my friend, Gary Rossington of Skynyrd, lived in Jackson and that maybe, just maybe, I could talk him into coming out to the gig and maybe, just maybe, sitting in. Well, at that time, Gary was a husband and a dad and a regular guy, so he jumped at the opportunity to get out of the house for a few hours. No arm twisting needed.

The band was not intimidated at all, and the jam was pretty damn good. Gary sat in for a couple of sets and then headed home. Before he left, he invited all of us to his house for a barbeque the next day. Gary and Dale were great hosts and seemed really happy to be around some good ol' boys from the South. The beer flowed and stories were rampant and maybe a little weed was smoked . . . I don't remember!

We spent several more days in Wyoming. We did some sightseeing, ate some great food, and actually went skiing. I was a formidable intermediate/advanced skier, but my friends from the Tangents had never been on skis before, and they picked one of the hardest mountains on the planet to learn.

Sipsack and Duff had talked each other into going to the top of the lift after about three short runs on the "bunny" slopes. Now keep in mind, we were all dressed in blue jeans and barely adequate coats. The top of the lift was freezing cold and windy as hell. It was a short-lived day on the slopes. I had skied down off the top and stopped to wait on them to get to me. I waited and waited and thought about heading on down and catching the lift back up to where I'd left them, when about that time, I see Sipsack coming over the ridge, walking, with his skis thrown over his shoulders. Duff made it down on skis, but needless to say, they'd had enough.

Our trip to Jackson Hole was one for the history books, and we were all glad we survived the mountain, the after-show parties, and Gary Rossington's cooking.

One other time, I met the Tangents in Telluride, Colorado, at the Fly Me to the Moon Saloon. It was much more sedate but a ton of fun, all the same. The Tangents are no longer a band, regretfully. Charlie Jacobs passed away several years before we lost Duff, which left an enormous hole in the Mississippi Delta music and art scene. I attended Duff's funeral in Ruleville, Mississippi, and like most of the Tangents' gigs, it was standing-room only. Rest in Peace, old friends.

The Tangents. L to R, Fish Michie, Duff Durrough, Bo Diddley, and Charley Jacobs.

Sandie and I visited Dale and Gary on several more occasions, and each time was more enjoyable than before. On one such trip, Dale and Gary were chomping at the bit to play their new music they had been working on. They had named their group the Rossington Band, and their first effort was called *Returned to the Scene of the Crime*. It was excellent music and good to know they still had that fire burning in them.

They had a few dates booked and asked me if I would like to come along with them. I didn't hesitate. They played a show at the Dallas Hard Rock Cafe and Boz Scaggs came out for the show. I was thrilled because I had been a longtime fan, and his song "Loan Me a Dime" always moved me. He was a super nice guy.

Later in that same time frame, they played a show at the Fox Theater in Atlanta as opening act for Kansas. It was an incredible show, and they were received well by their old "adopted" hometown.

Billy Powell and Leon Wilkeson came out to that show and,

afterward, came to the hotel where we were staying. They were there for the purpose of trying to convince Gary to reform Skynyrd for a short tribute tour to coincide with the ten-year anniversary of the plane crash. Gary was adamantly against it and let them know, in no uncertain terms, it would never happen. Things got really ugly that night, and luckily, no one came to blows, but it was a close call.

I didn't think much more about all that until my next trip to Jackson Hole, when Gary told me he had been talking with Charlie Brusco, an Atlanta promoter. There was definite interest, nationwide, in a Skynyrd tribute tour. Gary said, "I'm this close to saying yeah, but I just want to be sure it's done right." I asked him what his concerns were, and he said he didn't want it to be as crazy as before—all the drinking and drugging needed to be controlled. He then said, "Pauly, if you will come out with us on this tour, I will say yes."

Of course, I'd never done anything like that before, but that didn't seem to matter—to either of us. Thirty-two shows in thirty-two cities, then Gary and Dale would go back to the Rossington Band. I was hired as Security and that was the position I held for a couple of legs of the Tribute Tour, until the band and management realized I did a whole lot more. That's when I was promoted to Tour Manager.

And So I Became a Tour Manager

ong story short, thirty-two shows came and went. Every show was played to a sell-out crowd in some of the largest arenas and amphitheaters in the country. The tour could not have gone any better. The Rossington Band opened all the shows on the Tribute Tour. Muscle Shoals' famed Swamper Jimmy Johnson came along to mix sound for them, as his son Jay was a band member. There was no drama, no drugs, and very little drinking. Everybody got along. It was crazy to think it could continue like that, but it did.

The next leg of the tour did as well as the first and, again, no drama. It was almost too good to be true. Later on, as more dates were booked, I came to find out, it WAS too good to be true.

The road is a hard life, although most fans think it's a constant party. You wake up in a different town every day, not sure what day it is or what town it is sometimes. My road motto was: *never get off the bus before you have a cup of coffee and have looked at the Book of Lies*. And, oh yeah, *put a hat on that "bus hair."* You'll save yourself a lot of funny looks.

At Jim Carson's gathering in Nashville.
L to R, T-Bone, Al Cocorochio, Billy Copeland, Jim Carson, me, Norris, MJ, Rogco, Steve.

The guys in this picture traveled extensively together throughout North America and seldom had a cross word.

Gloria and Buddy at our home.

Scrapbook

After the writing portion of this memoir was completed, I then faced the difficult task of selecting photos to represent various portions of my life. All the pictures were taken with real cameras— not the ones that everyone has in their pockets today. Selections were limited, but still difficult. Invariably, some of my family, my Delta friends, my road friends are not included here, and I wish I could include each and every one. However, limitations of time and opportunity prevent that. Please know, you all matter to me. And enjoy the photo collage!

Me and Alden Byrd sharing a moment over
"Green Eggs and Ham."

L to R, Tommy Lampkin, brother Carl, Billy Guy.
The pumpkin is either Anne or Mary.

Willie, Dad, and Alec.

▲

L to R, Carla Turk, Patsy Carollo, Nancy Jo Morlino (Leland Girls) and my brother Carl.

◄

L to R, Marshall Pyle with video cam, me and Carl, and Carl's son Alec at his feet, sitting beside the stage.

Photo courtesy of Craig Reed

▶

Mama, Charley Pride, and Daddy. The way mama is looking at him, I know Daddy said something very funny.

My brother Carl and Robert McClellan.

My favorite uncle, Thomas Lampkin.
My Uncle Tom was a card. Very mischievious!

▲
L to R, my daughter Terrie, brother
John, me, cousin Steve, brother
Carl, and cousin Tommy

◄

Me and Mama

Tiffany and Natalie Abraham and
Granddaddy Carl.

My favorite Aunt Marjorie

◀
Brothers Carl, John, Paul in the front. Miller and Kitty Abraham in background. We had a wonderful childhood thanks to Daddy and Mama.

Paul Abraham. "While my guitar gently squeaks." ◄

Stoneville friends. L to R, Charles Walker, Ameil Stewart, Junior Moore, John Thomas Greenlee, Phil Cefalu, Sam Walker. ▼

L to R, George, Custer, Johnny Van Zant, Paul, and Craig
This Japanese gentleman owns a kimono shop in Tokyo,
and he caters to all the musicians who come through.

L to R, Randall Hall, Billy Powell, Carol Bristow,
Dale Rossington. And 50,000 of our closest friends.

Slydog with Cali friends, Big Anthony and his sister Cindy Cecil.
Photo courtesy of Scott Cecil.

L to R: Llary Rowell, Leon Wilkeson, and Craig Reed.
Always fun!

◄

My two favorite band leaders, Ed King (Skynyrd) Terry Shelton (BRC)
Photo courtesy of Norris Sherrill.

Me and Billy Ray Cyrus at a bike rally.

►

L to R, Arti Pyle, Charlie Daniels, Gary Rossington, Billy Powell, and Johnny Van Zant. Not a keyboardist in rock more important to their band than the great Billy Powell.

At Mt. Rushmore with Slydog.
Back, L to R, Norris, T-Bone, me, Michael Joe, Roger, Billy.
Front, L to R, Bob Workman, Barton Stevens, Steve French.

Leon Wilkeson at the Omni in Atlanta, New Year's Eve, 1980.

"Gimme 3 Steps"
My view most concert nights!

Jay Johnson and his dad, Jimmy, an original Swamper and
producer extraordinaire. At Epcot.

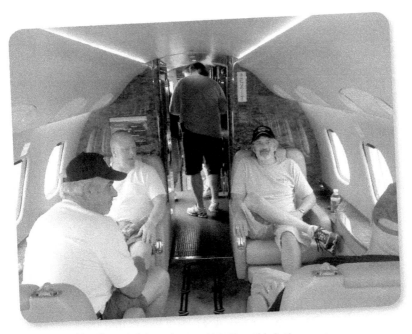

Heading north in a chartered jet. Now, this is the way to
tour. I sure loved this part of my job.

Me with Billy Ray's biggest fan ever, Mrs. Polly Barfield!

L to R, Steve Morse, Billy Powell, Ellen Powell.

Terry Shelton, Oliver North, Norris Sherrill.
Photo courtesy of Norris Sherrill.

Taking a break from rehearsals in Jackson Hole, the
Skynyrd boys try their hand at snowmobiling.

Randall Hall attempts a hijacking with a water gun. Billy
Powell is amused. We always had fun.

L to R, Michael Joe Sagraves, Terry Shelton, Billy Copeland, Charlie
Daniels, Billy Ray Cyrus, Dave Moody, Norris Sherrill.
Sean Hannity Freedom Tour.
Picture courtesy of Norris Sherill.

Randall Hall and Billy Powell as
ballerinas on a street in Japan.

Paul doing some damn good tour managing.
L to R, Rogco, me, BC, Charlie Brown, BRC, MJ, T-Bone,
Norris, and Bob.

L to R, Ed King, Johnny Van Zant, and Gary Rossington.
Emerald Studios, Nashville - Endangered Species sessions.

L to R, Sean Hannity, Billy Ray Cyrus, and Jon Voight.
Photo courtesy of Nancy Hughes.

Me, Chocolate Myers, and Billy Ray Cyrus at Bristol Motor Speedway.
Picture courtesy of Caron Myers.

◄

Me and Killer Beaz at
Charlotte Motor Speedway.

L to R, Gary Rossington, Killer Beaz, Johnny Van Zant,
and Hughie Thomasson.

PART FOUR

HIGHLIGHTS AND LOWLIGHTS
(In no particular order)

USA TO LONDON

It had been a long flight, and too many drinks were spilled down some of the band members' throats. Gary was well lit, and it seemed that he and Dale were having some sort of a disagreement, which was not that unusual. Her expression was a scowl, and his was one of anger. I never knew what had happened to make them both so unhappy, but with each step, I could tell he was going to explode at any minute.

We had walked probably a hundred yards into Gatwick Airport toward the customs agents. Dale had walked out ahead, and I was pulling up the rear to make sure I didn't lose anybody along the way. She was laying out her carry-on on the table for the agents to go through. She turned around to Gary, who was maybe ten feet behind her in line, and growled at him to hand the agent her passport that was in her makeup bag, which he was carrying.

Without a thought of the consequences apparently, he slung the case toward her and hit her—not hard enough to physically injure her, but aggressive just the same. Seeing this, the customs agents turned their attention to him.

It took some talking to keep them from hauling him off to jail, but somehow we persuaded them to let us take responsibility for him. We made it out of the airport without another incident. We made sure the two were in different vehicles for the ride to the hotel, and separate rooms once we got there.

I thought things had calmed down enough after a while, so

I went to check on Gary at just about the time he threw his room service order of fish and chips out of his hotel room door against the opposite wall. The food slid to the floor, and the smell was atrocious. Before long, the entire hall smelled like rotten fish. This time, I just turned around and walked away. Add all that to the airport fiasco, and I figured it was time for someone else to babysit these two.

Welcome to England, Yanks! Now go home! I'm sure that's what the person who had to clean up that mess was thinking. Heck, I was thinking it too. And the tour was just beginning.

For the record and in defense of Gary, traveling with a spouse on a rock-and-roll tour has to be the hardest thing in the world to do. Even when my wife came out for a visit, she and I would always bicker about me having to work and not paying enough attention to her. An impossible situation for me, and I know it had to be tough on the prez and first lady.

As we ventured on through Europe, things didn't get much better. Gary called me one night when we were in Munich to say he was at the airport and was going to fly home unless I found him something to offset the beer he'd been drinking—namely, cocaine. My answer to him was go ahead and get on the plane, because there was no way I was going to jeopardize my freedom for him.

He said, "You're fired, then."

I said, "Fine by me,"

Well, he finally sobered up enough to realize that it was going to be my way or the skyway. When he was sober, he was easy to deal with, and when he was drunk . . . well, thank God for Craig Reed. He was always able to bring Gary back down to earth, not so much because of his sage advice, but because he'd been there on that plane and he understood. It was a real demon they fought every day.

A few days later, I was walking along the Rhine River, enjoying the beauty of the city of Koblenz, Germany, with its castles and medieval architecture. It was a gorgeous day, and I decided to go back to the hotel to see if some of the band or crew wanted to grab a bite to eat at the bazaar that was just down the street.

I walked in the front door of the hotel, and to my shock, I saw our piano player, Billy Powell, standing at the front desk with blood all over his face and hands. I freaked! I ran over and asked Billy what happened, and he literally couldn't talk to me. He was running drunk and had no clue where he was or what he was doing. In broken English, the desk clerk asked me if this guy was with my group. I confirmed it and asked what the hell happened to him.

The clerk told me Billy had wandered into the parking structure underneath the hotel and couldn't figure out how to get back out. He stumbled around down there until he got so exasperated that he broke the glass on the fire alarm and pulled the handle, cutting his hand in the process. Within seconds, he was found, and his mission, although ill-conceived, was accomplished.

We had to pay the hotel to replace the glass on the alarm, and I had to talk the manager out of pressing charges against Billy, which was actually pretty easy. He was a Skynyrd fan, and now he had a story for the ages.

The next day was show day, and we were playing at the Loreley festival. As we were loading the hotel van to take us to the gig,

Gary started giving Billy hell for his antics, and a fist fight ensued, which I jumped in the middle of and stopped before it could go too far. I literally sprawled myself across Billy's chest so he couldn't move. Gary calmed down, and we went on to our show that was on the other side of the river, high on a bluff. It was a magical place, and by the time we got back to the hotel, all the ill feelings were forgotten. At least for a while.

———————

I'm not sure what got into these guys, but it seemed they liked to wait till we got out of America to pull their craziest stunts, like the time the hotel manager in Tokyo knocked on my door and told me one of my people was smoking pot in the room. The manager was going to call the police.

Two words: Paul McCartney! He once was arrested for having a small amount of pot on him in Tokyo.

Don't ask me how I talked this manager into not calling the police, but I did . . . and saved Mr. Rossington's ass once again. It was always something with those guys. I should have been a lawyer! After a few years on the road with them, I already had enough credits for a degree in psychology. I was a pretty damn good mediator too.

Looking for Leon

Looking for Leon was an almost daily occurrence on the road. Leon Wilkeson welcomed one and all into his hotel room, and they would talk him into going to a club or their house or almost anywhere at all. Billy called them Leon's Cling-ons. Leon also had a really hard time every year when the twentieth of October rolled around. He, like all the survivors, felt like he had cheated death on the plane that night in the Mississippi swamp, and he was truly haunted by that.

I remember one October 20th when we were in Concord, California, at the Concord Hilton. We had the night before off, and we hung out at the hotel. All of the hotels we stayed in would usually comp us a suite since we were buying forty-plus rooms a night. It was my night for the suite, which turned into two nights with the day off. I was sleeping like a baby at about six in the morning when my phone rings. It was Johnny Van Zant.

He said, "Paul, Leon is in the room next to me, and he's either trashing his room or somebody's killing him."

I jumped out of bed and ran down to his room. Right away, I could feel a rush of air coming from underneath the door, so I knew from experience that was not good. I knocked and knocked, and I heard Leon fidgeting with the deadbolt and the safety chain.

He finally got the door open, and as I got a look inside the room, I was blown away at the amount of damage one person could cause. Leon was looking at me like the cat that ate the canary.

I asked him what had come over him, and he said, "Ronnie, Steve, Cassie, and Dean."

I told him I understood. He was very apologetic, but my only concern was for his welfare.

The bathroom was demolished, mirror and all. There were glass and wood splinters all over the floor of the room, and there was a couch hanging halfway out the window. I told Leon to gather up his things and then I put him two doors down in Craig Reed's room. As I was leaving him, I heard him say, "My per diem is in my desk drawer. It's three hundred dollars."

I went back in Leon's room, and there was no desk in the room. I looked out the window and saw it lying on the roof below, already surrounded by workers, who had been working on an AC unit. The desk was demolished, and the drawer was hanging out, empty.

My next move was to contact our tour accountant and the hotel manager to assess the damage and pay the hotel so we could keep Leon out of jail. The bill was in the thousands, which was promptly taken out of Leon's draw.

———

There were other times when Leon would be sleeping so hard in his room we had to take the hotel door off the hinges to see if he was even in there. Nobody had cell phones in those days, so we had to rely on the hotel phone. Leon was a "salt of the earth" kind of man. He would have a drink or two and maybe a line or two, but he would never talk bad about anybody and seldom ever cursed. I remember one day I was frustrated and said goddammit, and Leon chastised me, "Don't say that, Paul. If you feel like saying it, do it this way, *"Got dandruff, and some of it itches."*

That was Leon.

On the bus, we would be watching a movie, and Leon would

have the remote and rewind the tape about every five minutes, saying, "Did ya see that? Now you got to watch close. Did ya see that? Here, let me back it up again." He would do this until Billy Powell would scream in his thundering voice for Leon to give him the remote.

———

We were flying into Jackson Hole in the dead of winter. Gary had a friend who owned a village of cabins called Togwotee Cowboy Village. It was just north of Jackson and just southeast of the lower entrance of Yellowstone Park. Our plan was to rehearse for an upcoming album, and Gary felt like this would be a great place to do it in.

On approach to the landing, the visibility outside was nearly zero. It was snowing so hard I could barely see the wing of the plane. Leon could obviously tell I was a little nervous, and he began to poke me continuously in the leg, saying, "We're not going to crash. We've already been in one crash. What are the odds?"

Well, Leon was right. I flew with Skynyrd all over the world, and other than a few incidents at airports, we always made it safe and sound. We stayed in Jackson for ten days or so. The band worked real hard, and we took a day off to snowmobile across the road in this huge playground of snow-covered hills and dales.

We all got suited up and were waiting on Billy Powell across the road so we could take a picture on our snowmobiles with the Tetons in the background. The next thing you know, here comes Billy barreling across the road, driving right past us, down the hill, around the bend . . . and gone. Our guides FREAKED out and told us to stay where we were.

They took off after Billy, and his sled tracks led right to a snow-covered creek bed within which he was buried. They dug him out, tied a tow rope to him, and pulled him right out of the creek.

Needless to say, Billy's day of snowmobiling was short lived. Our day sure wasn't, though. We had a blast being a bunch of rednecks out there acting crazy in the snow. We stayed out there a few hours, and it wore us all out.

A great night's sleep with a lit fireplace, and it was back to work the next day. After our time in Jackson Hole, we prepared for the flight back to the South. We all got to the airport on schedule, which was a miracle anytime that happened.

Everyone was through security except Leon, and he had more baggage than anyone. The security officer was going through his luggage when Leon put his last piece on the conveyor belt a big, black plastic garbage bag with his dirty laundry in it. The officer threw up his hands and just waved him on through.

———

There was another time, flying into Anchorage, when I found myself seated next to Leon. A few weeks earlier, a volcano had erupted near the bay that we had to fly over on the approach to Anchorage, and the pilot had warned us about possible turbulence.

Now, I've flown hundreds of thousands of miles in my life and I've experienced turbulence, but none like this. The first bump felt like the plane had plummeted a thousand feet, and then it started bucking like a bronco.

Leon's drink was completely out of the glass and hovering near the ceiling, and then it came back down and most of it went back in the glass, believe it or not.

The wings were flapping wildly, and I fully expected them to fall off. I looked down to see a bay filled with icebergs, and I figured that was where we were destined to end up. It was, by far, the scariest flight I have ever been on.

I looked over at Leon and then across the aisle at Billy Powell. They were totally unfazed by the turbulence. Billy was actually laughing at me. I guess my fear was written all over my face.

Once again, it was Leon saying, "Don't worry. Paul. You're in good company." And it can be said that, yes, I was. When we finally touched down, I released the chair arm from my death grip and looked out the window, shocked to see a moose standing fifty feet from the runway.

We were in Japan riding back toward Tokyo after doing a show in Osaka. And when I say "riding," I mean we were flying low on a Bullet Train, power poles flying by, Mount Fuji there and gone, rice paddies, four-story driving ranges. I was sitting back, enjoying the view and marveling at the idea that I was actually in Japan riding on a Bullet Train. Billy Powell was sitting across from me, asleep. A porter came up to me and asked me if I knew Mr. Leon.

I said, "Yes . . . what's wrong?"

He asked me to come with him and bring my credit card. I was like . . . *Oh boy!*

Leon was in the lounge car—imagine that. And he'd been setting up the folks at the bar for the entire time we were on the train.

Leon said, "Paul, can you bail me out here? I spent a little more than I have."

I asked, "How much did you have?"

"Well, I have these three one-thousand yen notes. I thought sure that would cover me, and I was trying to get rid of all my Japanese money before we left the country."

I asked the bartender what he owed.

"Forty-one thousand yen."

At that time, that was about three hundred twenty US dollars. A small price to pay, all in all, for a friend like Leon. The little scamp!

As I've mentioned, Leon was the salt of the earth. And I'll say it again and again. One day, in Sacramento, Leon and I were walking around outside the Arco Arena, and he spotted a little bird wrapped in what looked like fishing line. It was struggling, and Leon was afraid this little bird was going to die right in front of him.

He bent down, picked the bird up, and spent five minutes unwrapping the line from its wings and feet. The bird stopped struggling. It must have known it was in good hands.

When Leon finally got it free, he set it back down on the sidewalk and said, "Fly away, little bird." The bird stared up at Leon for what seemed like a minute.

Leon Wilkeson and his son, Lee Lee.
Photo courtesy of Lee Wilkeson.

I asked Leon if he thought the bird was injured. He said, "No, he's all right."

Then we watched as the bird hopped twice and flew away.

That's Leon! He was the best. And he is greatly missed by his friends and family.

That night, Johnny Van Zant sang "Free Bird" for the first time. Everyone considered it an omen, me included. Before that night, he would put Ronnie's hat on a mic stand, center stage, and leave the stage until the song was over.

BILLY POWELL

A nyone who knew Billy Powell knew of his long battle with alcohol. It was really a horrible addiction for Billy, who, when sober, was one of the nicest people in the world, but when he was drinking, he would black out completely and, at times, become belligerent.

Believe it or not, it never affected his playing. We were in Japan for six shows in ten days, and Billy, bless his heart, was in blackout mode the entire time, but never missed a note in any of the shows. It was actually amazing.

He had the classic symptoms of an alcoholic, always hiding what he was doing from everyone around him and ordering vodka in a water glass through room service.

One time, I watched a room-service waiter go to his room with nothing but three water glasses on his tray. After the guy left, I knocked on his door. Billy opened it, and I could tell he hadn't been to sleep at all. I "preached" to him a little and then asked him what he had done with the other glasses of vodka. Looking remorseful, he reached under the bed and pulled out two full glasses of vodka. He gave them up to me, and I thought maybe he was on the way to trying to sober up. No such luck. He just ordered more.

After that, I would instruct the front desk in all the hotels to always send his room service to me, and I would deliver it for them. That worked for a while, but an alcoholic finds ways of getting around obstacles.

We had been off the road for a few weeks when I got a call from band management telling me that Billy was holed up in a hotel in Jacksonville and wouldn't come out for anybody. They wanted me to fly to Jacksonville, rescue Billy, and take him to my house in Tennessee. I accomplished this with the help of Brian Evors, Skynyrd's stage manager, who actually was the one to coax Billy out of his room. The two met me at the Jacksonville airport.

Billy was agreeable to spending some time at my house, which was way out in the country, at least eight miles from the nearest liquor or beer store. This intervention would go extremely well for Billy, and I was feeling a certain degree of satisfaction for giving him the opportunity to sober up.

And sober up, he did. He would spend the days watching TV, or we would go down to Mike Estes's house (about a hundred yards away), where Billy would put down the piano parts of our *Drivin' Sideways* project. I was encouraged because he never asked for anything. Sandie and I didn't drink, so it was cold turkey for Billy. I don't recall any DTs or withdrawals. He was just normal Billy Powell, or as normal as Billy Powell could be.

I used to visit Billy at his home on Swamp Fox in Jacksonville. His demeanor at my house was much the same as when he was home, so I knew he felt comfortable and right at home. Hell, I even gave him my most valued possession: my remote control. His mind was occupied with other things besides alcohol, though I'm sure an occasional toke helped too.

One day, after about two months with Billy at my home, I had to drive into Nashville for some errands and was gone several hours. When I got back, I saw a car out in the field in front of my house cutting donuts. I couldn't believe what I was seeing.

Now, Billy Powell has never had a driver's license, but there he was, behind the wheel of a rental car, having a ball. Unexpected and uninvited, a friend from Texas had come by my house on the way to North Carolina, and with him, he had a pocket full of valium and a case of Budweiser. Billy was well into a relapse.

Keep in mind, Billy had already been at my house for nearly two months, clean and sober, and well on the way to recovery, albeit maybe short-lived. In an instant, it had all gone out the window. All our hard work and sacrifice down the drain because of a "friend" who had interfered. After that incident, I told Billy he would have to go back home because I wanted my life back. I put him on a plane to Jacksonville the next day, and my days as a substance-abuse counselor were over and done.

Actually, once Billy got back home, he did great. With a wonderful woman like Ellen there to support him, he stayed sober for quite some time; however, once we got back on the road, the demons reappeared with a vengeance. I was certainly willing to do anything to help him out, but push had come to shove and I'd had enough. I still loved him like a brother, but the responsibility that was laid in my lap was beyond friendship. But you know . . . I would do it again tomorrow if he were only here to ask.

When Billy Powell passed away, I was on the road with Cyrus when the news came, and it was a hard day, for sure. I will always have fond memories of Billy and his antics and his hardy sense of humor. He was the funniest guy on the road, hands down. We played Yahtzee for hours, watched *The Three Stooges* and *Popeye*, and passed many an hour on the bus, rolling down the road. I'm sure brother Carl and Billy have reconnected in Heaven, and they are both still talking about the bass Carl caught off Billy's dock at Lake Asbury on one of his visits to Jacksonville.

Billy Powell was a real joy to share that part of my life with. He probably cared more about me than anybody in the band. I spent many hours standing behind him, marveling at his piano playing. Although Skynyrd was known as a "three-guitar army," Billy Powell's keyboard work was essential to their sound, and he was absolutely the best rock pianist in the business. Since I started writing this book, Billy has come back to life for me. I listen to his solo on "Call Me the Breeze," and can still see his fingers tickling those ivories. I miss Billy. He was a true friend.

Thomas "Artimus" Pyle

I first met Artimus Pyle on an elevator in New Orleans on the way to a Rossington Collins Band (RCB) Mardi Gras concert. He was on crutches after breaking his leg in several places in a motorcycle accident. It was my understanding he was scheduled to play drums for RCB until the accident, and the band hired old friend Derek Hess, or as Billy Powell called him, Hectic Mess.

The next time I saw Arti was in San Francisco as we were beginning rehearsals for the Lynyrd Skynyrd Tribute Tour in Oakland, California. As I was going into the hotel, a young boy, maybe ten years old, walked out of the hotel with a skateboard under his arm. His dad was walking beside him and said, "Now, Marshall, you be careful out here on these streets." It was San Francisco streets he was talking about. Most of us have seen these streets in movies or images, if not live. No place for a ten-year-old hellion on a skateboard. The dad wore a warm-up suit and had rather short hair and a mustache. I absolutely did not recognize him until later when he was introduced to me in the van heading across the Bay Bridge, where the van broke down in the middle of rush-hour traffic. (That's another story for another day.)

The man was Artimus Pyle, or Tommy, as his family called him. Everyone can recall the picture of Artimus on the now infamous original *Street Survivors* album. He looked like someone out of the Old Testament, and suddenly I was seeing him looking almost like a preppie. He had brought along his two sons, Marshall and Chris, for the first leg or two of the tour. Arti never had any problem bringing more people into our traveling entourage. At one time or another, he had two or three members of the Israeli army and a Rabbi traveling on the bus.

Artimus was a bit of a daredevil, and he was always game to do something crazy to enhance the production. Two New Year's Eves in a row, Skynyrd played a show at the Cow Palace in San Francisco, and Bill Graham always went all out for the band. The first show, in 1989, Arti was taken to the far end of the Cow Palace and up on the roof. He dropped in through a hatch door, and the crew rigged him into a little bi-plane with the words "Mylvyn Skyrydyr" on the sides. At one point, the band and management had thought about using the name to avoid the "lawsuit" cloud.

Anyway, Arti was in the plane, and it was moving slowly down toward the stage with spotlights on it, and the wheels hit the stage at the stroke of midnight. Cool effect, but the next year's production was pretty cool too.

After "Sweet Home Alabama," Arti climbed the lighting truss rope ladder into an actual horse saddle on a huge Jack Daniels bottle that was hidden behind a curtain. He rode it down from the truss, and at the stroke of midnight, the bottle tipped down and poured tens of thousands of ping-pong balls on the stage. The crowd went wild!

Arti was a real joy to work with. He never asked for anything special and was not interested in doing cocaine, as some of the others were, and he did not drink—or, as I found out in Portland, Maine, he *could not* drink. We were gathering at the bus, and I had walked back in the lobby to check on our accountant, who was settling the hotel bill. Artimus had been in a mood all day and, apparently, had a drink or two in the bar. As we were all done at the front desk, in walked Artimus through the lobby, karate-chopping every crystal coffee table in the lobby, leaving behind a trail of destruction. Automatically, the accountant reopened his briefcase and pulled out the credit card.

I followed Arti out the front door and had him back against the front window of this fine old hotel, trying to calm him down and find out what had triggered all that. He was like a man possessed and would not listen to a voice of reason. He slammed his elbow against the front window, which must have been twelve feet tall and at least twenty feet wide. It shattered and fell straight down. Luckily, no one was hurt. The glass literally fell all around us. We were held up at that hotel for an additional three hours, trying to settle the damages with the hotel.

The only other instance when Arti lost control happened at Kingswood Amphitheatre outside of Toronto. The distance from the hotel prohibited us from going back after sound check, so we hung out at the venue. Artimus, for reasons unknown to me, decided to have a little drink of champagne that turned into a bit more than a little drink. He was agitated most of the afternoon, and no one could talk to him.

A few hours later, which seemed like an eternity, the band took the stage. We had been using two drummers on the tour for some time because of Arti's injuries affecting his stamina. During the set, I was watching Arti from the wings and he seemed to keep getting angrier and angrier about something. He picked up his snare drum and threw it over his head onto the stage behind him. He grabbed a tambourine and started hitting his ride cymbal with it until it broke, and he flung a piece of the tambourine and almost hit Dale, the head Honkette and Gary's wife.

Gary looked at me over his shoulder and made the head motion that told me to get Arti off the stage. I ran out to his drum riser in the middle of the song, grabbed him from the back, and bear-hugged him off the stage. Kurt Custer, our second drummer, hopped on stage and never missed a beat.

Arti tried several times to go back, but by that time, I had help and he succumbed. He and I sat on a slope behind the stage as he cried and ranted. As the band played "Saturday Night Special," he cried that it was his song and he didn't get credit for it. I knew Ed and Ronnie had written the song, but you never know the circumstances surrounding who was "in the room" at the time.

After the show, it was a logistical nightmare trying to get everybody on their respective buses and back to the Four Seasons, Toronto. After we finally arrived at the hotel, I went to my room to pack for the overnight bus ride to our next city. I got a phone call from one of the crew saying that Artimus was trashing his room, and Johnny and Gary were trashing a suite. It was all hell breaking loose for the Skynyrd boys that night.

At the end of the ordeal, Artimus had played his last gig with Skynyrd that night, and we were asked politely (or maybe not so politely) to never return to that hotel property or any other Four Seasons property in the world.

It was a sad night for me, because I really liked Artimus, but he had a vendetta of sorts against a couple of band members and he lost control. And I say . . . so freakin' what? Who in that organization had not shown his or her ass at one time or another? It should have been written off and forgotten. Artimus should still have his gig even after that crazy choice he'd made. He deserved the right to lose it every now and then. All of them did. So did I.

The saddest part was, as we were pulling out of the hotel parking lot, I saw Marshall Pyle, Arti's youngest son, inside the glass door of the hotel, watching us leave. That was August 2, 1991, and I haven't talked with Artimus since that time. He is currently in the news again, being sued by the Skynyrd organization for a documentary movie he is ready to release about the truth surrounding the plane crash and the demise of the original band. Artimus has gotten a raw deal from the Skynyrd organization since that fateful night in Toronto, and in my opinion, should be allowed to do whatever he wants with his story as long as it's truthful. And knowing Arti like I do, it would be an honest and very poignant depiction. His story needs to be told.

KILLER BEAZ

The Tribute Tour rolled through Birmingham, Alabama, on the ten-year anniversary of the plane crash, and I was standing in front of the hotel, loading the band and management on the two fifteen-passenger vans sitting under the canopy. I noticed a guy easing over closer to me.

This guy was a sight. He had on a black sports coat with black and white cowhide across the shoulders, and he wore matching cowhide boots. I was thinking, *Oh Lord.* I was deeply into what I was doing, so I didn't want to get into a heavy conversation with this dude, but onward he came.

"Hey, man," he said. "I'm Killer Beaz, world-famous comedian. I'm doing a show here in town tonight." He was a fast talker, and he asked me how I liked his jacket and boots. I told him I thought they were stylish, and went back to counting heads in the vans. He said, "It's Panda." He got my attention then and I laughed out loud. He asked, "Who you got here?" I told him it was Skynyrd, and he was completely dumbfounded then. He said he was a huge fan and had been playing Skynyrd music for a long time. I told him we were headed out to do a show, but we would be back at the hotel for a while after the show. I asked him to have his show videotaped, so we could see his act. After our show, I was sitting in the lobby with some friends when Killer Beaz walked back in with VHS tape in hand. He walked up to me, gave me the tape, and asked me if he could meet some of the band members. I told him Leon was in the bar and all of them would be coming down to get on the bus shortly. We hung out and talked for a few minutes. I found out he was originally from Jackson, Mississippi, and was living in Mobile, Alabama, touring throughout the South, doing four to five shows a week.

As we rode out of town that night, we plugged in the VHS tape. For the next hour, we laughed our asses off, and Killer Beaz became a fixture with all of us. A few months later, I found out Killer was performing at Zany's in Nashville, and I would not have missed it for the world. The next day, he came out to my house in Dickson County for a visit. We remain friends to this day, and I try to see him as often as possible.

Opening Acts

I was always drawn to our opening acts because I wanted to make sure they were getting everything they needed to put on a great show. In the world of bands and the egos that are attached, a lot of times the headliner can dictate the number of lights or the amount of the stage the openers can use. Ronnie Van Zant used to tell his production manager to give the openers whatever they wanted and more, since it all added to the overall quality of the show. Made good sense to me, so I carried on his tradition by making sure our openers were happy. Gary Rossington also felt this way, and he always made it a point to ask me to make sure the openers had everything they needed.

Other openers through the years were the Doobie Brothers, 38 Special, Charlie Daniels Band, Ian Moore Band, and Hank Williams Jr., although Bocephus really hated opening for anybody, he conceded after a certain incident in Legend Valley, Ohio. So, Hank insisted on closing our show that was way out in the middle of nowhere.

He learned a hard lesson that day for any headliner who followed Skynyrd's "Free **Bird**" on the stage. Once the band was off the stage and it was handed over to Hank's crew, the crowd had started to move toward the exits. I mean a huge cloud of dust was rising from the rear of the field and well over half of the audience had left. We played many more shows with Hank, but that never happened again. Lessons were learned! But not by everyone . . .

like the Stones in Knebworth, England, or ZZ Top in Memphis, or the Who in every city they visited with Skynyrd. No band, no matter how established they were, could follow Skynyrd on the stage with the crescendo of the entire set as it builds to a head and explodes with the fourteen-minute rendition of the greatest rock song ever written. Just an impossibility. Yet, some still tried.

FANS

Skynyrd fans were definitely a loyal bunch and I got to know a lot of them quite well. Along the way, I met some awesome folks and still stay in touch with them via Facebook and email. I can't name them all, but some were unforgettable. For Skynyrd fans, they had to overcome the description in a little joke I'd tell before I could really get close to them. The joke?

What has sixty feet and ten teeth? *The front row of a Skynyrd concert!*

One particular fan from Little Rock, Ed Slater, worked for Kroger, one of the largest supermarket chains in the country. Ed always brought cakes out to the band when we came to town. One of his very best was in the shape of a white grand piano he presented to Billy Powell. We loved seeing him coming because we knew his cakes were straight. Point of fact: bands usually won't accept anything like that because there are some crazy people out there. Ed's cakes were eaten down to the crumbs. He also is a limo driver and has some wild stories to tell. We'll wait for his book on that one. He's also a friend of Guy Santucci, one of my neighbors when I was growing up in Leland.

Ed was recently telling me about an old veteran friend of his whom he would meet and take to lunch weekly. The old guy relished these meetings with Ed because, sadly, his family paid very little attention to him. That's why I love playing music at the old folks' homes. Our elders need our attention. I wish everyone would be inspired by Ed Slater. His friend passed away recently, but unlike a lot of vets, he passed away knowing that someone really cared for him.

<hr />

I'm not sure what caused it, but about the time "Gimme Three Steps" came around in the set, there would be trouble brewing in the audience. I guess it was partly due to the close proximity of festival seating, partly due to the alcohol . . . who knows for sure? But I saw hundreds of fights.

For example, every time Skynyrd played in Philadelphia, the City of Brotherly Love, there would be a huge fight right in front of the stage. The band would get distracted to the point they would actually stop playing. Johnny would throw water on the melee, only making things worse. Not only would they *not* stop fighting, but then they were slipping and sliding on the concrete floor.

The security guards at most venues were well trained and knew how to quell these fights, but I was thinking they were actually enjoying it sometimes. I'd actually had to go into the pit myself and tell Security to move out, that we would take over with crew members and stagehands. It always worked out.

We did this once in an outdoor venue in Missouri, and the stage was at the bottom of a slope. Gravity was a bitch that night. People kept getting smashed against the barricade, and it was actually getting scary.

I recall this one little skinny girl—and I mean skinny. I kept telling her to let me help her over the barricade and then she could move to a place that wasn't so crowded. She agreed, and we made it happen, but it wasn't a hot minute before she was right back against the barricade. Well, hell.

I just let her be until she took off her shirt and was attempting to throw her bra on stage. I turned around to see the band members laughing their asses off, and I turned back around with the intention of begging this girl to PLEASE put her shirt back on. About that time, I was smacked hard in my left eye. The girl had thrown her bra onstage and, with her follow-through, hit me right in the eye. I was pissed, but I laughed it off. That was my last time telling Security to leave, my last time trying to do it myself . . . and the only time I got a black eye on tour.

———

Another night in Peoria, Illinois, in an indoor hockey arena, about the same time in the set, a huge fight started up about five feet from the front of the stage. Gary Rossington kept looking at me to go take care of it. I kinda shrugged my shoulders and stayed put. Then, right in the middle of the song, Gary unstrapped his guitar and basically threw it at his guitar tech, then he tapped a security guard on the shoulder and stepped right off the stage with the guard's assistance.

Big Wally Smith and I both leapt off the stage right behind Gary. The fight stopped, and Gary pleaded with those guys to quit. It was surreal. We didn't need to be there, but Gary had accomplished what he wanted.

We helped him back onto the stage; the band started exactly where they'd left off, finishing the song and the set with no further incidents.

I really don't know what Skynyrd music does to people, but I can't count the number of times things like that happened.

I guess it had something to do with the way those guys used to fight with each other.

Dirt Tracks to Superspeedways

A ll my young life, I loved going to the stock car races at the local dirt track. The sounds and the smells were intoxicating to this young boy. My "across the street" neighbor, Ray Bernie Carpenter, was one of the people I loved to watch race. He was daring, and he was one hell of a driver. He used a "sissy ball," for lack of a better word, on his steering wheel, and he drove with his right hand while holding on to the door jamb with his left. He was fun to watch.

Bobee Polasini was one of the more serious drivers out there. Not only was he a great driver, but a great engine builder, and to this day, a great friend. He will do anything for anybody. Bobee and his wife Carol are big fans of "That'll Do" and are always the first couple on the dance floor. I treasure their friendship.

Ellis Palasini started out racing on the dirt many years ago and progressed to the asphalt half-mile circuit pretty fast. His son Butch and his daughter Kat had always been good friends of mine. Butch asked me to come along with them a couple of weekends for racing in Jackson and Mobile on consecutive nights. Ellis became a legendary race-car driver in these parts.

I remember once in Jackson, Ellis's car stalled and needed a push. Butch jumped in the truck and, for some reason, Ned Ruggeri, Phil Cefalu, and I jumped in the back, sharing the truck bed with a fifty-five-gallon drum of nitro. As we pulled up on the banking and started to push Ellis off, the truck bumper kinda slid to one side of the race car, and the truck's right front tire went up on the race car's left rear wheel, and for a split second, the truck was on two wheels. A friend of ours in the stands said he could see the oil pan of the truck. I guess we were too dumb to be scared, but we came very close to being the headline in the next day's newspaper. It wasn't until we got back in the pits that I realized how lucky we were that the nitro hadn't fallen right out of that truck. Actually, I have no idea why it didn't.

My love for racing stayed strong through the years, but it had moved from the small-time ovals to the big-time superspeedways. I had only been to Talladega one time, and I got the feel of what NASCAR was all about. I never dreamed that my next visit to a racetrack would be as a guest of NASCAR at the Daytona 500. Columbia Records put out a compilation album called *Hotter Than Asphalt*, all songs about NASCAR racing. Lynyrd Skynyrd took top billing on the album with a song called "White Knuckle Ride." I encouraged Johnny and the band to get into NASCAR, because, at the time, a great deal of Skynyrd's fan base was at the track or watching it on TV.

The sport was growing in leaps and bounds, and I really wanted to see them cash in on it. Johnny Van Zant, Mike Estes, and I represented Skynyrd at the 1996 Daytona 500 in support of the *Hotter Than Asphalt* project. Other artists that came in for the promotion were Mark Collie and Killer Beaz, a comedian whom Skynyrd had a little history with. That's a whole 'nother story, as a Southerner would say. He did a song called "Save Up," and his backup band was Lynyrd Skynyrd; we all sang the chorus: "SAVE UP." There are other artists on the album, but I can't remember exactly who represented them at the racetrack. They are Joe Diffie, Waylon Jennings, Alabama, Tanya Tucker, Little Texas, Tracy

Lawrence, Hank Jr., and Mark Collie. We met King Richard Petty that day, and he graciously stopped after he ran to his motorhome during the race to relieve himself to take a picture with us. He was larger than life. His wife had asked us to come visit her during the race . . . and there he was, totally unexpected. That was the first Daytona 500 I had ever attended, and, needless to say, I was completely blown away by the spectacle of the whole event. I became a solidly hooked NASCAR fan.

Racing Songs

Mike Estes and I were neighbors in the country about thirty miles from Nashville, and when we got home, we decided to sit down and write some songs about racing. We were inspired! Our first song was "The Intimidator" about seven-time champion Dale Earnhardt, which Billy Powell put a smoking hot piano solo on. We played the demo for a few people in Nashville, and they were pretty much all saying it was good stuff. I remember Vince Gill was in the room when it was being played at the Sound Kitchen in Franklin, Tennessee, when I was there with Bad Company. He stopped in his tracks and I could tell he was really getting into the song. After it was over, he said, "Only thing wrong with that song is I didn't write it. It's great!"

With this coming from Vince Gill, I felt really encouraged about the project we had begun, and Mike and I wrote five more songs in a short time. We wrote a song called "Ballad of Junior Johnson," a former moonshiner who brought R.J. Reynolds to the table and fattened up the drivers' purses. Ed King played a hauntingly beautiful guitar solo on this song, which, other than his solo on "Sweet Home Alabama," and maybe "Swamp Music" and a few dozen others, is my favorite piece of Ed's guitar work. From this point on, NASCAR was a viable and increasingly popular sport. "That's Just Racin'" is about a day at the track when almost anything could happen—*expect the unexpected* is the theme of the song. "Boy Wonder" is about a young up-and-coming driver at that time called Jeff Gordon. Dale Earnhardt tagged him with the name Boy Wonder, after Batman's Robin. It was obvious that Dale Earnhardt loved this kid, but he treated all drivers the same. He was a good-natured instigator, constantly pranking people. Jeff learned to love Dale too.

"What Else Would I Do On Sunday" is a song in which I wrote most of the story line, and Mike made it work in a song. It's about a guy that wants to go to the race at Rockingham, but is a little scared to confront his wife. Finally, his friends talk him into it and he tells her, "Like it or not, I'm going." She says, "Go, but you better have your butt back here Monday morning for work." Well, as NASCAR weekends often go, the guy had way too much fun, and he was late for work Monday morning. Matter of fact, he was late for work Monday afternoon too. Oh well.

At this point, the 1996 season was ending, and it was looking like Terry Labonte was going to win the championship. Mike and I sat down and wrote "The Iceman," which is Labonte's nickname, in about thirty minutes. Labonte drove the number 5 Kellogg's car, and we came up with some cool lines like, "Powering down the backstretch in that Kellogg's Chevrolet, Rooster out there crowing on the hood." After we had written six songs, Mike put together a band with some old friends and between him and the other three band members, they wrote four more songs. "Nascar Diehards" is about the wild and crazy people who fill the grandstands and bleachers every week to romp and stomp and cheer on their favorite driver. "Asphalt Angels," which was written by the bassist, is a poignant anthem for the drivers who had been killed "on that old blacktop road to nowhere." "Yellow

Flag Blues" is about just that: caution flags and how they change everything in a race. The last song for the CD was a song that Ed King and Mike Estes had written to be pitched to country artists in Nashville. It was originally called "Redneck Romance," but the name was changed to "Racetrack Romance." It was about a couple who pulled for different drivers, and it created quite a stir usually, since the drivers were Rusty Wallace and Dale Earnhardt.

With songs in hand, we went to the last race of the season at Atlanta Motor Speedway, where in fact, Terry Labonte won the championship. The Monday morning following the race, the track traditionally put on a big spread called the Champion's Breakfast. Our friend with Speedway Children's Charities, General Tom Sadler asked us for the demo of "The Iceman" and when Terry came in, they played it start to finish. There were many drivers and crew members there, and among the guests was Franco Harris, the man who made the "Immaculate Reception" when he played for the Steelers. I shook his hand that morning as I had shaken his quarterback's hand some years earlier when I'd met Terry Bradshaw at Keystone Ski Area in Colorado.

We got to do a lot of cool events with NASCAR in the next couple of years. The band played at the racetracks before the race, actually on the track. Also, we were invited to the inaugural race at the Texas Motor Speedway, where the band got to play for a drivers' gala. Dale Earnhardt and Rusty Wallace were at the front tables, and they were entertained with songs that were written about them. Neat stuff. The *Drivin' Sideways* CD was released in 1997 on Eagle Records, an independent record label in Nashville. We had good distribution in stores and on Amazon. Being that we were giving a portion of the proceeds to a NASCAR charity, we placed the CD in several racetrack gift shops, where they absolutely could not keep them in stock. I was in Los Angeles, walking down Hollywood Blvd., and turned into Tower Records. Flipping through the titles, I ran across three *Drivin' Sideways* CDs. I was floored.

The problem with the CD was that our indie label was totally not expecting the demand for the CD and dropped the ball on distribution. Mike and I took the CD back from them, and we began to sell it online at www.cdbaby.com, who shopped it to iTunes and several other sites. We did marginally well with it for several years, and then sales dwindled, and we forgot about it. The album is still listed on the sites and has digital downloads available. We sold every physical CD we had made.

More Recollections from the '90s Era

There was an instance when Lynyrd Skynyrd and crew were on some interstate in America, before the advent of the cell phone. Two "unnamed" members on different buses were having a beef with each other for several days, and this particular night, they were jawing at each other over the buses' radios.

I figured someone better call their bluff before it spilled over into the shows, or worse yet, spilled some blood. I made the drivers pull over to the side of the highway and told these two angry ones to go at it. They pushed and shoved, but no blows were passed. One was scared, and the other was glad of it, I guess. We had our moments!

Mark Collie sponsored an annual event at the old fairgrounds racetrack in Nashville, and he had asked for a representative from the Skynyrd band to drive a Legends car in the celebrity race. Owen Hale, Skynyrd's drummer at the time, was the only one willing and available, so I accompanied him to the race. The race benefited the Diabetes Foundation that Mark, who is a diabetic, had worked with for many years.

The race was always a big deal in the Nashville music community and had plenty of draw power with not only music stars, but movie and TV stars as well. The real treat for me was the number of NASCAR legends who would show up to support Mark's cause. I got to meet and talk with Bobby and Donnie Allison, the two brothers who had founded the Alabama Gang from Hueytown, Alabama, and raced for many years. They were friendly and down-to-earth, and while they were sharing some old war stories with Harry Gant, I got to sit and listen. It was a great experience for me, a moment in time I will never forget.

At the same race was the Petty hierarchy from King Richard on down to Kyle and his son Adam. This family has been the "first" family of racing for many years and had high hopes for son Adam in the racing business. In 2000, Adam became the first fourth-generation driver to race on the Winston Cup circuit, and just forty days later, he died in a qualifying run at Loudon, New Hampshire. I'm glad I got to meet Adam that day in Nashville. He had a great future, cut so tragically short.

The absolute highlight of the day was being in the same "space" as my favorite movie star, Paul Newman. Everyone had been told not to approach him for autographs, and I certainly did not. I did, however, catch his eye and give him a nod and a big thumbs-up. He returned the gesture, and that was my brush with a true legend.

I had a similar experience with an old nemesis of his, Steve McQueen. He was staying at a Holiday Inn in Greenwood, Mississippi, while he filmed *The Reivers*. Some friends and I drove over to possibly catch a glimpse of him on the set, but we saw him at the motel instead. He stepped out of his room and nodded to a bunch of star-struck teenagers, then went immediately back into his room. That was plenty enough for us!

The Legends Race went well, but not without its accidents.

Owen flipped his car during the race and Rudy Kalis, a local TV sports guy, actually had to go to the hospital and be treated for a head injury. Among the stars who raced that day were Vince Gill, Ronnie Dunn and Kix Brooks, Aaron Tippin, and Keith Urban. Dean Sams, the lead singer for Lonestar, won the event.

———

Lynyrd Skynyrd, 1994

We were in Berlin, Germany, at the Intercontinental Hotel after a show, and I was getting everybody prepared to travel. That night, we would drive through Germany into France and on to Paris. I had called everybody to alert them the bellman would be coming for their luggage and to expect a knock on the door. I also told them that after the luggage was gone to come on down to the bus and we would head out.

I had not been able to reach Leon, which was not unusual. I had a good idea where I could find him, though, so I headed for the bar. He was there, talking with some long-haired, tattooed guy and showed no sign of getting ready to leave. I said, "Leon, the whole band will be waiting for you to get your shit together so we can leave. I need you to go up and pack and get back down to the bus in twenty minutes."

The greasy guy sitting with him said in an English accent, "Leon is talking to me, and he will go when we're done. Don't you know who I am?"

I said "I don't really care who you are. Leon is holding up the whole band, and we don't play that around here, and if you have a problem with that, we can talk more some other time maybe, but right now, I need Leon."

Unfazed, he said, "I'm Lemmy Kilmister."

I still really didn't have a clue who he was. I said, "Okay, now let's go, Leon."

Leon got up and came with me. I asked him who that guy was. He said, "Oh, Lemmy is the bass player and lead singer for Motorhead."

I said "Ooo-kay." I still didn't know who the hell he was. And sure didn't care, but I did get Leon on the bus in time. We were on the way to Paris.

Our first day in Paris was a day off, so we got out of the hotel and saw the sights. We had two limos pick us up, and our first stop was the Louvre, where we spent several hours touring the famous museum. We saw the *Mona Lisa* and Venus de Milo, and Michelangelo's David. The building was originally built as a fortress and palace for King Phillip II, and after King Louis XIV chose to build his palace in Versailles, the Louvre remained as a place to display the Royal Collection, and was opened as a museum in 1793.

We next went to the Eiffel Tower and while some of the band chose to climb the tower, Gary and I opted to remain in the car and have a "production meeting." I wasn't crazy about climbing the tower. I got enough exercise just keeping up with everybody.

We then went to Montmartre, which was a strategic hill used by Henry IV's artillery during the Siege of Paris, and where the Basilica of the Sacre'-Couer now stands.

After all this, most of the guys were tired from all the sightseeing and wanted to go back to the hotel, which they did. A couple of the crew guys and I decided to go to Jim Morrison's grave. We figured we may never get back to Paris again, so we took advantage of it.

It was Johnny Van Zant's birthday, and we were playing at a

1,000-seat nightclub in downtown Paris. The club was completely packed from wall to wall, and the band was hot as fire, as usual . . . and so was the temperature inside that club.

I never noticed any friction on stage that night, but after "Sweet Home Alabama," the band left the stage and went to the dressing room, and that was when things got a little crazy. We usually had several rooms backstage, but that night we only had one room. Everybody was crowded in, and Johnny was pretty drunk on Jack Daniels. I remember he and Randall Hall had some words, and a shoving match started.

Big Lew, a member of our management team, and I jumped in the middle of it, broke it up, and sent the band back out to finish the show—"Free Bird," and then out the door. All went well until we got back to the hotel, and it started up again. It was all because Johnny was drunk and had no cocaine to neutralize his drunkenness. He took a swing at Ed King; Ed threw up his left hand defensively, and Johnny hit Ed's hand and broke the finger he uses for his slide.

Johnny also took a swing at Big Lew.

Finally, Johnny went to his room, and we thought all was well until I got a call from Big Lew saying Johnny might be trashing his room and having an argument with his wife, who had come to France to be with him on his birthday.

I got out of bed and went down to Johnny's room, where there was a huge ruckus going on inside. I knocked, and his wife opened the door, screaming at me to call the gendarme to arrest Johnny and take him to jail.

By that time, I was well inside the room, and Johnny turned his wrath on me. He picked up the luggage stand and flung it at me. The steel bar hit me across my shins, and Johnny came running at me like an out-of-control bull, or at least, a little bull.

I did what any Delta boy would instinctively do. I nailed

him with my right fist smack in the eye. As he was going to the floor, I lifted him up with a punch to the ribs. About this time, the gendarme did not have to be called; they were knocking at the door.

Johnny told them to take me to jail because I'd assaulted him. His wife was begging them to take Johnny to jail instead, but I convinced them that it was all over and that I would take responsibility for . . . whatever. They went for it, thank God. I wouldn't want me or Johnny to have to spend time in the Paris pokey, but that night, he learned what it was like to get hit by someone with an experienced right fist.

I figured I would get fired for it, but actually, I received a bonus. We were flying from Paris to Heathrow Airport in London the next morning, and I was standing on the sidewalk at the front door of the hotel getting everybody on the bus for the ride to Charles de Gaulle Airport. Johnny and his wife walked out the door, and she gave me a nervous smile . . . but a smile was good. Johnny, on the other hand, told me he would get me back, even if he had to creep me. I said, "Bring it on, Johnny. If that had been your big brother Ronnie getting on your ass last night, you probably wouldn't be able to make this trip today. And just so you know, your new hotel alias is Jack Damage. Johnny B. Good no longer applies."

Gary and Dale came out next, and Gary said he wanted me to book him and Dale on a different flight than Johnny's. I said, "I have a better idea, because I ain't wild about flying with Johnny either. Our show isn't until tomorrow. Why don't the three of us have the bus drop us off in London? He has to deadhead back anyway." Gary agreed.

That turned out to be the most enjoyable trip I have ever had on a tour bus in Europe. We drove from Paris to Calais and took the ferry across the English Channel. We stopped at a little fish-and-chips shop and had the best I have ever eaten. All in all, it was a great day with Dale and Gary. They did have their good moments. I thanked Johnny for the great day when we met him at the hotel. Johnny had a definite problem with Jack Daniels. He looked like a man possessed when he was in the throes of that stuff.

Johnny was just one of those people, and we have all known one or two that fit the description: a mean drunk who will pick on anyone nearby. His brother Ronnie was the same way. And Papa V (Lacy) was the same way too. Now, I never saw Donnie get riled up about anything, but I only saw him in good situations. I imagine he carries that gene, but it doesn't show up that often.

Adversity and the Van Zant family were a bad mix.

There was a particular day in Atlanta when I had to intervene between the Van Zant patriarch, Lacy, and the Atlanta Police Department. Lacy was out with us, and he had decided to bring Ronnie's old truck out on tour and would sign autographs and take pictures with fans by the truck.

We were staying at the Ritz Carlton, and Lacy and Gene Odom were trying to find a place to park the truck until they were ready to go to the venue. Shortly, I got a call from the front desk telling me the trailer hauling the truck was parked in a loading zone, and asking if I could please have it moved.

I called Gene, and he and Lacy went down to deal with it. Well, Lacy got into a shouting match with the cops, and they were just about to haul him and the truck away. I got there just in time to save Lacy from the handcuffs. So, not only did I have responsibility for the band and crew, now I had an irate old man in the mix. I loved Lacy, though. He was one of those old guys who had a million stories to tell, and he sure didn't mind telling them to anyone who would listen.

One other time in Knoxville, Tennessee, Johnny apparently thought he could fly. He was in a two-level suite with kind of a winding stairway. He and his wife were arguing about something again, and Johnny leaped off the stairway about five steps from the bottom. When he hit the floor, something in his back gave way, and he went down.

We took him to the hospital in Knoxville, where he was x-rayed and given a back brace for ruptured or fractured disks in his lower back. He did the shows, but he was in extreme pain throughout the remainder of the tour. I kinda got a kick out of it. All the times that boy had caused other people pain, it was his turn. *What goes around comes around.* I'm not sure who came up with that saying, but it was certainly appropriate in that case.

Johnny wrote a song about it called "Devil in the Bottle," but I don't think he was listening to his own words. Check out the lyrics online. You'll see what I mean.

Sweet Sweet Connie

Any tour that has graced the stages of Little Rock, Arkansas, has come in contact with or at least shouting distance of Connie Hamzy, the groupie who was immortalized by Grand Funk Railroad in "We're an American Band." Connie was damn proud of her chosen "profession," which was more like a hobby, since she didn't get paid. She showed up early in the morning to "visit" with the various crew members who were game, and from them, she found out the name of the tour manager so she could hit him up for passes when he arrived with the band.

I knew better than to give her passes—our tour had several wives out with us, and it just wouldn't be the smart thing to do.

So, we drove up this one day, and I saw Connie. She was already wearing a working pass. I started asking crew members who might have given her the pass, and when I didn't get an answer, I just blew it off and hoped she would behave around certain band members. I wasn't going to piss off the crew by taking her pass, so what was done was done.

All went well until the last note of "Free Bird" stopped echoing through the night air. I watched one of the band members easing around the crew bus, and I figured he was sniffing Connie out. He stepped on the bus, and within seconds, his wife stepped on right behind him.

I was outside, so I didn't see or hear what went on inside the bus, but in a few minutes, they both came off the bus, and the wife was livid. She went to the production manager and demanded he tell her who gave Connie the pass. It was ugly. She threatened to have the entire crew replaced if someone didn't fess up.

Lips were sealed. I was sure their bus driver got an earful that night. I was just happy to have them off my bus, and I was never more relieved to get out of Little Rock than I was that night. If I ever saw Sweet Sweet Connie again, it would be too soon . . .

Well, wouldn't you know it? When I went to work for Cyrus (more on that soon), we were on the bill with Montgomery Gentry at the Little Rock Riverfront Park Amphitheater, and on the way to the gig, the guys wanted to know if I knew Connie. I relayed the story of the Skynyrd fiasco to them. They asked me if I thought she would remember me. I said I don't know how or why she would.

We pulled up backstage, and the first person I saw was Connie on rollerblades, and she had a young protégé in tow. She was teaching this younger girl the ropes, I guess, because she was getting on up there in years. I got off the bus, and once again, Connie already had her passes.

She shouted, "Paul!"

I'm like, *Oh, Lord.* She wanted to meet Billy Ray, and I said, "No way. No how! If you knew how much trouble you caused me before, you wouldn't even ask." It was a lot easier to deal with her that day since there were no wives to contend with, and not only that, Billy Ray's guys had a hell of a lot more sense than that particular Skynyrd guy.

———✦———

James Taylor, Nashville, 1994

We had a good day in the studio by finishing four basic tracks, and Gary Rossington asked me to hook us up with some James Taylor tickets at Starwood Amphitheatre that night. I made a call, and we were set. We left the hotel, and Gary asked me to stop at the liquor store for some Jack Daniels. I begged him not to make me do that, but he would not relent. It was Johnny, Gary and Dale, Steve Lockhart, and me. I sent Steve in to get the Jack, and Gary and Johnny were in the back of the van getting tuned up for the show. I had a sense from this point that the night was going to be one to remember.

By the time we got to Starwood, Johnny, Dale, and Gary had dipped into the Jack. By the time James Taylor came on, Gary was lit up. About halfway through the show, the music made Gary have a religious experience, and he got up, walked to the barricade, and started to climb over it. I ran up and brought him back to his seat.

After the show, we went backstage to get to the van and head back to the hotel. James Taylor was outside of his dressing room, so Gary went up and mumbled a few things to him, which at that point were totally incoherent.

As Gary walked away, I noticed James had a very puzzled look on his face, and he asked his manager who that guy was. His manager didn't know, so I tapped James on his shoulder and told him it was Gary Rossington of Lynyrd Skynyrd.

It was like a veil had been lifted, and he nodded his head

and said, "Oh, I see!!" Years after that night, I had the chance to remind James Taylor of this instance, and he actually remembered his encounter with Gary Rossington.

After we got back to the hotel, Johnny, Gary, and Dale continued to rave. It was getting really late, and we were staying at the Residence Inn in Brentwood, Tennessee—there were a lot of business folks there who depended on the peace and quiet so they could be ready for meetings and such the next day.

There would be NO peace and quiet that night. Johnny and Gary got in an argument about who was going to get the last drop of Jack. I went to Gary's suite to calm them down and then headed back to my room, weary and looking forward to some sleep. I was just about to doze off when I heard a big bang on the side of the building where my room was. I looked out the window, and Big Lew yelled at me to come and help. Johnny and Gary, at it again.

I got out there and grabbed Johnny, and Lew grabbed Gary. They both were acting like the West Jacksonville rednecks they have always been—only now they were rednecks with cash, a dangerous combination. They both were struggling, and Lew and I would not let go. About that time, the sprinklers came on, and all four of us went down. Fists were flying, but, remarkably, no one got hit. Everybody headed back to their rooms, including me, and . . . a knock on my door.

It was a Brentwood police officer, who had been called by someone saying there was a disturbance. Hoping this young man was a fan, I told him the truth about who it was and that it was all done now. Indeed, he was a fan, so he let it slide, but he came back several times during our six weeks there. I also invited him to the studio as our guest. We were covered from then on. We never had any more problems at the Residence Inn.

Circa 1994

While Skynyrd was recording a new record at Emerald Sound Studios in Nashville, my wife and I were moving from Mississippi to the Nashville area, so a perfect place to stay until we had our loan closing was at the Residence Inn. Sandie was already working at a TV station in Nashville, and I would go to the studio each day to run band members back and forth from the hotel to the studio.

I called Ed King from the studio to tell him I was on the way to get him. When I got to the hotel, I figured I had a few minutes to let my two golden retrievers out to go do their business before I took Ed back. I walked in the room, and the phone rang. It was Ed telling me he was ready and he was walking out to the van. I looked at my dogs and apologized. "Sorry, guys. Gotta go. Be back shortly."

After making it to the studio and back to the hotel in an hour or so, I headed to the room to check on the dogs. It had been totally trashed. I guess I'd made them mad when I left so abruptly, and they'd made me pay—about four hundred dollars or so in damages.

Not only did my dogs chew holes in the blanket on the bed, they ate the little arm doilies off the couch. All four corners on the coffee table were thoroughly gnawed.

Thankfully, the next week, we closed on our house, and the dogs were back in the country where they belonged.

———

Southern Spirit Tour, 1994

Late spring and early summer of 1994, I was asked to act as tour manager for the Southern Spirit Tour that featured 38 Special, Marshall Tucker Band, Fabulous T-birds, and Barefoot Servants. With 38 Special was Johnny Van Zant's brother Donnie, Don Barnes, Jeff Carlisi, Larry Junstrom, Danny Chauncey, and Bobby

Capps. All great guys who never seemed to let stardom go to their heads, unlike some other folks I've known. Feel-good music always.

Fabulous Thunderbirds featured Kim Wilson and Stevie Ray's brother, Jimmy Vaughan. Although they were a great band, they never really rang my chimes.

Barefoot Servants. Many people have made comparisons between Jon Butcher and Jimi Hendrix in the early stages of Jon's career, who has been quoted as saying, "Being black and playing a Stratocaster created certain inevitable comparisons, particularly in the early days."

To me, he just rocked. It was so much fun to listen to his set each night. He worked the stage from one side to the other, all the time killing guitar leads. For a while, he had a fabulous bass player who played full-time for an Atlanta band called Mother's Finest, probably the tightest group ever assembled, which only had regional success. Wyzard was his name, and that's exactly what he was on the bass guitar.

A few days out, another bass player showed up, and I was immediately starstuck. His name was Leland Sklar, who was best known as James Taylor's bass player. Starting out, Taylor asked him out for a few gigs, and they both figured it would be just that—a few shows, and not much more. As it turned out, Lee stayed with James Taylor for most of his career, yet still found time to work with a seemingly, never-ending roster of artists through the years, from Toto to Jimmy Buffet, from America to Jackson Browne, from Clint Black to Reba McIntire, on and on and on. When you have a few hours to spend, go online and Google "Leland Sklar." It may bring back some good memories for you . . . oh, and I should mention Ray Charles in that roster! Leland Sklar was fun to watch and a joy to be around, and to this day, with the advent of Facebook, we are still connected.

But for all these bands and amazing entertainers on this tour, there was one that stood out, head and shoulders over all of them: the Marshall Tucker Band. Although they were a shell of what they once were, missing Tommy and Toy Caldwell, the two brothers' music still rang out with the familiarity and feel, as if they were all still there onstage. The voice of Doug Gray just flat made me feel good, so soulful and strong. Doug and I had some great talks and walks on this tour. Every day, when we pulled into a new town, you could tell the ones who had slept. Doug and I were always on the sidewalk and ready for a walk through the town. Doug was religious about his walking, and after that, I was too. In every town I visited, weather permitting, I would be the first one off the bus and heading out. To this day, I feel like I'm cheating myself if I don't go for a long walk every day. My dog, Buddy, feels like I'm cheating him too.

The tour was fun, but short-lived for me. I had to go back to my regular gig with Skynyrd, and after three weeks spent on the Southern Spirit Tour, I actually kinda dreaded it.

Meeting Dale Earnhardt, 1996

When Skynyrd was finishing up the album *Endangered Species* at Ed Hopson's home studio in Atlanta, I got on the phone with a friend, J.R. Rhodes, who worked as PR man for Dale Earnhardt. The NAPA 500 Winston Cup race was being held at Atlanta Motor Speedway the upcoming weekend, and I thought it would be cool if some of the Skynyrd guys went to the race. To make it worth their while, I contacted our friends John Boy and Billy with the Big Show out of Charlotte, North Carolina, and we came up with an idea to do some impromptu meet-and-greets at the track for fans that made up posters saying something about Skynyrd, racing, and John Boy and Billy.

We were all amazed at the effort those folks put into making the posters, and there were a bunch of them too. We rode through the infield in two black SUVs and would stop and get out when we would see a great poster. Then we would hang with the fans, and the guys would sign autographs.

When we wrapped up with John Boy and Billy, we ran into J.R., and he said Dale Earnhardt was doing a big media deal introducing his car for the Winston, the all-star race during Charlotte Speedweeks. J.R. had told Earnhardt that the Skynyrd guys were there, and Earnhardt wanted to meet them. We stayed at the track most of the afternoon watching the Busch race and ended up leaving before Earnhardt was done with his obligations.

On the way back to the hotel, Billy Powell was a little less than happy about not getting to meet The Man, but the next morning, we ventured back to the track, where we were immediately called to Earnhardt's car hauler. We were escorted through the hauler and given the million-dollar tour. We were shown all the extra parts, fenders, and even three or four engines, ready to be installed in a race car at a moment's notice. Above the lower compartment was a complete race car, ready to go if and when needed.

When we got to the back of the hauler, we were escorted into the drivers' lounge, where, bigger than life, was Dale Earnhardt, with a big old Southern grin on his face. We talked for a few minutes, and I gave him a copy of our demo of "The Intimidator" on *Drivin' Sideways*. Then Earnhardt asked us if we wanted to take some pictures of all of us together, so we all stepped out the side door of the hauler and posed for several pictures with The Man.

As we were leaving, our drummer, Owen Hale, said to Earnhardt, "Why don't you come out and jam with us sometime?" Earnhardt, without a pause or a second thought, said, "I tell you what . . . if anyone gets in my way today, I will jam this race car up their ass." He did win the race that day, by the way.

That day was one of the highlights of my life, and I will never forget my first encounter with Dale Earnhardt.

Lynyrd Skynyrd and Dale Earnhardt. This picture was taken right after Dale made his funny comment.

His gas man, Danny "Chocolate" Myers, introduced me to Dale as his brother, since we bear a striking resemblance to each other. Chocolate currently has a radio show that runs 11:00 a.m. to 3:00 p.m. EST on Sirius Channel 90. Give it a listen some time.

The last time I got to see Dale was in November 2000 at Atlanta Motor Speedway. I was there with Billy Ray Cyrus, who was scheduled to sing the National Anthem. As it sometimes happens, the race was rained out on Sunday, and an impromptu celebration of Darrell Waltrip's retirement from racing was held in the Media Center. I got to meet many other drivers at this get-together, and also got to take a picture of Billy Ray Cyrus with The Man.

Sadly, a few months later, Dale Earnhardt died in a crash at the Daytona 500, on February 18, 2001, a day NASCAR fans will never forget. Three weeks later, Billy Ray was asked to sing the anthem at the Bristol race. Billy Ray and I were sitting on the bus that morning, having coffee and watching the crowd file into the track. I saw one older gentleman with a number 3 hat and t-shirt, and I said to Billy, "It looks like that old fella really don't want to be here." At that moment, Billy and I wrote a song called The Man, which was about that man and Dale Earnhardt. The song was later debuted on Billy's TV show, *Doc*. I'm not sure I ever got paid for that!

Skynyrd Guests

Through the years, Skynyrd had quite a few celebrities who would come out to the shows. One of those was the man responsible for discovering the band, Al Kooper, formerly of the Blues Project and Blood, Sweat & Tears. He also played quite a bit on the first two Skynyrd albums as Roosevelt Gook: bass, Mellotron, and back-up harmony on "Tuesday's Gone," mandolin and bass drum on "Mississippi Kid," organ on "Simple Man," "Poison Whiskey," and "Free Bird," Mellotron on "Free Bird," backing vocals and piano on "Don't Ask Me No Questions" and "The Ballad of Curtis Loew" and listed as co-writer on "Cheatin' Woman." He had a long history with the band and would come out often while we were on the Tribute Tour.

One night, Skynyrd's manager at the time, Bill Graham, brought Carlos Santana to the show at Shoreline Amphitheater, and I learned a very interesting tidbit that night. As Bill was introducing Carlos to the band, he said, "Oh, by the way, when Carlos and I first met, Santana was a jam band with very little structure. I brought them the song, 'Evil Ways,' and it became their first big hit." I watched Carlos throughout the set and noticed how much he already knew the music. It was always fun seeing those huge stars get blown away by that awesome band onstage.

He wanted to jam that night, so he plugged into the spare amp with a spare Les Paul and proceeded to destroy the lead guitar solo when it came time for him to play on, "Call Me the Breeze." He's an incredible guitar player, but just not a Southern Rocker, and folks, there is a difference. He was a good sport, and hung out for a while after the show with Bill Graham, as much a legend as anyone on that stage.

The next day, we went to Bill's office in San Francisco, where he "laid down the law" to the band about the drinking and the drugs that had reared their ugly heads again. Such a great man! We lost him a year or so later when he left a show at Cal Expo in Sacramento heading back to San Francisco and hit some high-tension wires in the helicopter. A great loss for Skynyrd, and an even greater loss to the music industry and the fans who support it.

Many other artists jammed with Skynyrd onstage—Jeff Carlisi (38 Special), Greg Martin (Kentucky Headhunters) Charlie Daniels, Steve Morse, (Dixie Dregs, Deep Purple), Toy Caldwell, and more. I loved meeting all those legends. I never felt intimidated when I met someone famous. I just acted like I had known them all my life. I do wish I had asked for more pictures and autographs, but it just wasn't my style.

When Skynyrd was approached to do a Pay-Per-View broadcast at the Fox Theater, it was a "no-brainer" for them to accept. The artists lined up to participate in this historic event. They included Tom Keifer of Cinderella, Peter Frampton, Travis Tritt, Charlie Daniels, 38 Special, Bret Michaels of Poison, Al Kooper, Zakk Wylde of Ozzy Osbourne fame, and several others. It was a fabulous show and an unprecedented event.

Ahmet Ertegun, the famous label head of Atlantic Records, came with his entourage of beautiful women. He also came out to the show we did at Radio City Music Hall, accompanied by many of the same ladies. He was a nice old fellow, and I tried to take good care of him that night—ha! . . . as if he needed it.

The afternoon of the RCMH show, we were invited to Ertegun's office in Manhattan. On the way up in the elevator, as he always did in elevators, Leon started punching buttons. He usually liked to hit the alarm button to let people know he was coming, but this time, he hit the emergency stop button.

The elevator stopped between floors, and that was where we stayed for thirty minutes or so. And that night, as if on cue, the elevator wouldn't open to take us four flights up to the dressing room, and there was no way the band would go back onstage without a visit to the dressing room. So there we went: the entire band, me, and a few others up the stairway for four flights to the dressing room. The elevator was at least waiting on us to go back down, but this time, no one wanted to take the chance, so there we went, back down the stairs.

A Spinal Tap moment if there ever was one.

—————

Skynyrd was doing a show in Denver at Fiddler's Green Amphitheatre with the Doobie Brothers opening. It was so much fun to show up at the arena during their set and hearing songs like "China Grove" and "Dark Eyed Cajun Woman" ringing out in the night sky. This particular night was really special for me. I was standing behind Guitar World, enjoying the Doobies, and noticed that a few feet from me stood someone I had been watching play football, live, since I had been living in Colorado, but now I was seeing him live right in front of me. I never was much of a "gherm," but this one I couldn't let pass by without getting an autograph.

It was John Elway with his wife, Janet. I struck up a conversation with him by saying, "Hi, John. I live in the mountains over there, and I can't tell you how many times I've watched you play at Mile High." He acknowledged me and stuck his hand out to shake mine. I had him sign my current backstage pass, while I mentioned a Monday night game of the preceding year when the Broncos had played their arch enemy, the Oakland Raiders. I was sitting in the South Stands, probably the craziest place to sit for a Broncos game. It's where the Man in the Barrel hung out, and the beer flowed from the time the stadium opened.

I said, "You surely remember that game, right?"

He said, "Oh yeah, if you give me a hint. I remember all the games I've played in . . . to a certain point."

I told him the game was played in driving snow, start to finish. He asked what the final score was, and I said, "It was 23-20."

"Yeah, I remember."

I said, "Yeah, but did you know that every point was scored into the South Stands by both teams?"

He laughed and said that I'd stumped him on that one and he'd have to look it up.

I then said, "Dale Earnhardt and I had a conversation about you when I saw him at the Atlanta race. He said when he would go to Daytona and always end up in second place, he would think about the Super Bowls you lost and say to himself: 'Wait till next year.' When he won in 1998, he gave credit to you and your persistence for the win."

Elway seemed to enjoy that. "Wow! Is that the truth?"

"The gospel," I said.

I was walking on air for probably a year after that encounter. John Elway will always be one of my idols, and it was so damn fun to be able to talk with him, without feeling that I was bothering him.

Many thanks to him for all the memories he gave me during his career and on that beautiful night in Denver.

In March of 1990, I got a call from an old friend back in the Delta, and he wanted to get in the concert promotion business, so we did a few small shows in Colorado Springs venues and did marginally well. Well, it lit a fire in this guy, and his family had just sold a business, so he was itching to blow his money. The best way to end up with a million dollars in the promotion business is to start with two million. His plan was to build a concert-size nightclub in Tupelo, Mississippi, and he wanted me as a partner because of my expertise in the music business and my connection with Skynyrd. I invested no money, just a year of my life, and I told him I could get Skynyrd to play for the big opening.

Sandie and I had found a nice little house on a lake about five miles from New Albany, Mississippi, a thirty-minute drive from Tupelo. My "partner" and his beer-drinking wife moved to Tupelo, and we proceeded to look for a builder who could build our club from spec. Not only did we find a builder, but he had some acreage that was perfect for what we wanted to do. The contracts were signed, and the building went up, 16,000 square feet, complete with a thirty-foot horseshoe bar and a restaurant in the front. I spent countless hours pulling bullets and nails out of old cypress boards that we'd brought in from the Delta to use in the building. The boards came from old shotgun houses that we tore down; new brick houses were built in their place for the farm workers. It turned out beautifully. We built a forty- by twenty-foot stage and figured that would accommodate most any act we wanted.

As it always does when there is a deadline, it rained a lot and put us behind schedule if we wanted Skynyrd to open. The band was to start the 1991 tour in Baton Rouge, where they were headed when the plane crashed in 1977. We put on the finishing touches and finished it in time to have our house band try out the stage on a Wednesday night and Skynyrd played there on Thursday night. During the show, my "partner's" drunk wife told a waitress, "We have Lynyrd Skynyrd onstage. We can get anyone we want now. We don't need Paul Abraham." The waitress immediately told me what the woman had said and that made up my mind right then and there. The plan was for me to stay and get the club off the ground, but when I figured out that these people only wanted to build this place so they and their drunken friends would have a place to hang out, my plans changed. I legally disassociated myself with them and went on back out with Skynyrd. I never looked back. They lost the club after six months or so, and another owner took over. Today, the building is a huge funeral home, and people are dying to do business with them. A sad ending to what would have been a decent future if folks would just act right.

<hr />

Skynyrd had flown into Cincinnati for a show the following night. We got checked into a fine old hotel and got comfortable in our rooms when a major thunderstorm blew through and uprooted this huge oak tree on the front lawn. The power went off, and I looked out of my eighth-floor room to see the tree lying over the lines. It would take hours and hours of repair to find out why no emergency generator came on, so I jumped in the stairwell and went down to the front desk.

The sales manager was talking to this man who seemed familiar to me. Before I could get a better look at him, they disappeared into an office nearby. I asked the front-desk person about the prospects for getting power back. She said the power company was on the way to remove the enormous tree, so it should be a matter of just a couple of hours.

Well, ten hours later, there was still no air conditioning, but thankfully the windows opened. The front that brought the storm also brought in some cooler temps, so that was a lifesaver for us. Aside from all the noise the work crews were making with their lift trucks and chainsaws, it was a pleasant night. Lemons and lemonade comes to mind.

The next morning, with power restored, I jumped on the elevator and went down to talk to the sales manager about what they planned to do to accommodate us for the inconvenience. I can't remember exactly what she did, but it involved free room service for lunch and the comping of several rooms. I turned around and saw the man I had seen the day before, walked up to him, and without a second thought, said to him, "I bet you a hundred dollars you're Pete Rose."

He looked up at me and said, "Smartass!" But then a big old grin came over his face, and I finally exhaled.

I said, "You're right. I am a smartass. I just can't help it." He laughed again and we got to talking briefly. The fact that I was with the band Lynyrd Skynyrd came up, and a look of recognition came over his face.

He said, "I always loved that band. Where are y'all playing?"

I told him and mentioned I would leave tickets for him if he would like to come out. He had some meetings, unfortunately, and was pretty sure he couldn't make it. "But thanks anyway." We parted ways with smiles.

As I said before, I never "gherm" celebs for autographs or pictures, but he is one I really wish I would have asked. And my two cents here: let him in the Hall of Fame.

Thrown in Jail in Manchester, New Hampshire

Everyone who knows me knows I have somewhat of a smart mouth, never meaning harm, but I just like to kid around with people. Skynyrd was playing in Manchester in a huge park by the Merrimack River. While we were waiting for Skynyrd's slot to play, I noticed four or five rookie cops with no badges or markings on their blue uniforms, so I wandered over to talk to them and learned they were still in training. Nice guys, all in all, but I would find out later, they didn't like a smart-mouthed southern boy. The final notes of "Free Bird" were still ringing from the stage. The band came off the stage and went directly to the buses. The plan was to leave right away, head back to the hotel, clean up, and leave for the next town.

Well, best-laid plans went straight to hell when two cop cars blocked us in so we couldn't move the buses. I walked off the bus and politely asked the officer in charge if they could move the cars a few feet so we could get out. The nice officer told me, "Hell no. We're breaking down an operation, and as soon as we get done, you can leave. Now either we can lock you up, or you can move along until we are done." They were actually loading confiscated beer and liquor into the trunks of the cop cars. Anyway, I complied.

I went to the buses and told our drivers what was said, and they, as drivers get, were a little antsy to be on the road. I went to the back of the first bus and acted as a ground guide for the driver, and after about fifteen minutes of pulling forward and backing up, we cleared the bus, and it rolled onto the street. Then I started on the other bus, and again, after about fifteen minutes, we got this one cleared to leave as well.

Here comes the good part. As I was about to step on the last bus, my smart mouth overloaded, and out it came. The young trainees were standing near the back of the bus, and I hollered, "I hope y'all graduate." I closed the door behind me and walked into the front lounge. I looked out the window, and there were six or seven cops knocking on the door.

Well, one thing I learned in my first years with Skynyrd was to never, ever allow a cop on the bus. Certain smells may have tipped them off as to what was going on in the back lounge, so I stepped off the bus, where I was immediately put in cuffs and carted off to jail.

As I was sitting in that jail cell for a couple of hours, I had no idea what was going on outside. Gary, Dale, and Big Lew finally came to the jail and bailed me out about midnight. Some fan had called the local radio station and told them of the incident. Well, the station's phone lines lit up after they mentioned it on the air. Local folks were outraged that the cops had taken one of the Skynyrd family and carted him off to jail, and apparently the phones at the police station had been ringing off the hook too. When Gary showed up with bail money, they opted to let me out with no bail. No charges were filed for me being a smartass.

———

Dale Krantz

When the Skynyrd plane went down, it was the end of a short moment in musical history. The band arrived on the scene in 1973 and their plane crashed just four years later—not a very long period of time at all, but long enough for the band to write its own history. There was no doubt at the time of the crash that the band was on their way to being perhaps one of the top five bands in rock and roll, with other bands like the Beatles, Stones, the Who and maybe the Eagles. Their music was so completely unique from anything that had previously been written and performed, and their brand was stamped into eternity, although their creative life died October 20, 1977. No one could write the kinds of songs

Ronnie had written. Not Gary, not Allen, not Ed. After the crash, as the first couple of years passed, no one really wanted to play. Their bodies were battered and their minds were shattered from the crash, and they made a pact to never use the name Lynyrd Skynyrd again.

Gary and Allen began talking again about doing something. Their desire to create and play music had returned, and their discussions turned to who would sing. They were certain that anybody who handled the lead vocal duties would be compared to Ronnie Van Zant, and it would be a monumental task to find someone who could come close to what Ronnie had done for the band. He was the glue, the leader of the band, the captain of the ship. So, they began to think in a different direction. What if they brought in a female singer to handle the job? Although the comparisons to Ronnie would still exist, it would not be as demanding on a female, if she could come close to pulling it off.

Dale Krantz was a backup singer for 38 Special at the time. She had a strong voice and the knack to do a bit of writing. Gary, Allen, Billy, and Leon got together with Derek Hess on drums, and Barry Lee Harwood on guitar, both Jacksonville boys, and began writing songs with Dale. Dale's voice was exceptional, and she was just what the guys needed to get back out there and compete in the music business.

The first time I saw the Rossington Collins Band was at the Omni in Atlanta on New Year's Eve, 1980. I was blown away as were the other 20,000 people who filled the seats. People were so happy to see these guys back together, and the fact that they had a female singer worked like a charm.

The band experienced a couple of great years touring and getting back out where they belonged, but the same old evil things that haunt bands reared their ugly heads again and caused the band's breakup. Dale and Gary were married and moved to

Wyoming, and the Jacksonville guys stayed put. A few years later, Dale and Gary formed The Rossington Band and released two albums, while Allen Collins brought in Randall Hall and Jimmy Dougherty and added the other guys to form the Allen Collins Band. They released one album which was critically acclaimed, but not strong enough to keep them busy.

Finally, the band came back together for the Tribute Tour and Dale came along as the head Honkette. She also sang with the Rossington Band as the opening act for the entire tour. She and Gary worked very hard on the tour, but it was evident, after a leg or two, that the Rossington Band would be no more. I thought that was a great loss, because Dale was so good center stage, but the demand for Skynyrd dictated the end for their great band.

One special time I remember with Dale was when Charlie Daniels asked her to sing on his gospel CD, *Steel Witness*. I accompanied her to Mt. Juliet, Tennessee, to Charlie's home studio, and spent the day watching and listening to the genius of Charlie Daniels as he created songs with Dale's voice in mind. She nailed it. It was a really special day for me and for Dale. I don't believe Mahalia Jackson could have come close to the music Dale recorded that day. It was an honor to be a part of anything that Charlie Daniels had his hands in, which through the years, I'm happy to say, has happened quite often.

Parting Ways

During my last few years of working with Skynyrd, Rossington would come to me and cry over the cocaine situation, because he wanted it all gone for good, supposedly. I promised him every time I would see one of the drug-dealing culprits come around, I would make sure they didn't get close to the band. But about the time the next day rolled around, he'd change his mind, right back in that rut.

It's amazing to me that people still go see them. It's such a phony group of wannabe band members now . . . it has become laughable. What once was "all about the music" had morphed into "all about the money." Ronnie would have kicked the whole lot's butts, starting with Rossington and his little brother.

MICHAEL PETERSON

While I was out with Skynyrd, I had the good fortune of meeting Gary Falcon, Travis Tritt's manager, and out of the blue, I get a call from him asking me if I would be available to go out with a new artist he represented as tour manager. I told him, tentatively, yes, but I wanted to meet this guy first to see if we would get along.

The artist's name was Michael Peterson, and he had already enjoyed some success. He was signed with Reprise Records, and his debut single, "Drink, Swear, Steal & Lie" charted at No. 3 on the Billboard country charts. The second one, "From Here to Eternity," became Michael's first No. 1 single. Michael Peterson was named Male Artist of the Year by Billboard in 1997.

Michael and I met at his home in Franklin and hit it off right away. I worked for him through 1998, touring America as part of a tour lineup that included Clay Walker and the Dixie Chicks. Clay was the headliner, and the Chicks and Michael swapped out opening the shows.

Around the middle of the tour, Michael and the Chicks were both up for the Academy of Country Music's Horizon Award. Both acts were invited to a steakhouse for lunch with some local radio personalities and contest winners in Raleigh, North Carolina, where we all sat down at a big round table for a meal.

The girls talked about playing "Truth or Dare" on the bus. They sounded like they'd had a ball on their tour bus while we were on a "milk and cookies" bus. That's not to say a few beers or a glass of wine may have been tipped occasionally.

Michael was a member of a national championship football team from Pacific Lutheran University and had a quiet demeanor on the bus. The band members were great guys, but not what I had become used to with Skynyrd, which was actually a good thing, but it was kind of boring . . . in a good way. No drinking and drugging on that bus. Thank God.

The Chicks went on to win the award, and although they were an exceptional trio, I feel like Michael would have represented country music a whole heck of a lot better with his demeanor and huge talent. Who on earth could have predicted the Dixie Chicks' implosion?

When I first came on board with Michael Peterson, it was my first endeavor into the world of country music. I was excited to be a part of Michael's tour, because unlike Skynyrd, he was getting radio airplay on his singles. His music was refreshing and unique, compared to some of the other offerings on country radio at that time. Not only was his music enjoyable, but so was he. He was always pleasant and didn't seem to let the rigors of the road get to him. That speaks volumes about his character.

One thing that determines the success of any artist is his fan base. His base was made up mostly of ladies, and they all wanted to get as close to Michael as possible. It was easy for me to understand their attraction to him—a tall, handsome athlete with a talent for love songs. Whenever we rolled into a town, there would always be a group of ladies waiting for us to show up. Michael treated his fans with the utmost respect, as if they were old friends. We would hang out at a venue for hours so he could sign autographs and have pictures made.

As an artist and a musician, Michael was top-notch. His stage presence was remarkable, and his songs were impactful, especially

"From Here to Eternity." So many people came up to Michael to tell him that song was played at their wedding, and no stronger compliment for a song is needed. "Drink, Swear, Steal & Lie" was a fun song and always got a huge response from the audience, as did the covers he performed like "When You Say Nothing at All" and "Memphis in the Meantime." He engaged his audience with his speaking voice as well as his singing voice. Michael's legacy in the music industry may not be as strong as the Beatles or Garth, but it is definitely noteworthy because of the strength of the composition and his vocal talent. Although I only worked for Michael a short time, it was the least stressful and most enjoyable tour I had been a part of.

Michael continues to make music and released two more albums, *Being Human* and *Modern Man,* performing his shows in front of numerous military audiences and concert venues across the country. He is currently the music director and a lead vocalist for a fabulous new Branson show called *Raiding the Country Vault,* in which his hits are highlighted along with many other country hits played by some amazing musicians onstage.

Michael has a new album to mark the twentieth anniversary of his debut album with new versions of his biggest hits plus a few goodies from other artists like "Wichita Lineman" and "Friends in Low Places." I expect to hear from Michael in a big way before he hangs up his spurs. Who knows? Maybe he'll even ask me to tour with him again. I'd leave tomorrow!

PART FIVE

MY TIME WITH BILLY RAY

TOUR MANAGER NEEDED

A t the end of 1998, I was, once again, looking for a gig. I had looked into some local working situations and was prepared to make that move, when Ed King, Skynyrd's former guitarist and co-author of many Skynyrd hits, including "Sweet Home Alabama," called to tell me Billy Ray Cyrus was looking for a tour manager, and he had recommended me. I met Billy Ray some years earlier at Emerald Studios while Skynyrd was there recording *The Last Rebel* album. He rode in the back gate with Little Steven Van Zandt on the back of his Harley. I also met his band and my future best friends that day.

Ed set up a meeting for me at Singin' Hills Farm, Billy Ray's farm in Thompson's Station. While I was there, he hired me on the spot. It was the beginning of a great friendship. He is a genuinely fine person, and I enjoyed many years working for him and his family, his management, and his fans.

Presidential Election 2000

Billy Ray Cyrus had been a Democrat his entire life, and his late father Ron was a big wheel in the AFL-CIO and one hell of a nice guy. Ron was active in Democratic politics for many years and would have had a fit if he knew the turn Billy Ray took in the 2000 election. He recorded a song called "We The People," a patriotic song that was pitched to both candidates as a campaign theme song. Al Gore's people apparently didn't like the song and declined the offer. George W. Bush, on the other hand, jumped on it, and the song was played at every rally and event during the latter stages of his campaign.

The week before the election, Billy Ray was invited to an Al Gore fund-raiser at the Wildhorse Saloon in Nashville, which he and I attended. I have never been in a more uncomfortable situation. The Dems looked down their noses at both of us that night. We had a similar experience at another candidate's fund-raiser.

I walked Billy Ray up to the suite in a swanky hotel in New Jersey and knocked on the door. From across the room, the candidate looked at us like we were intruders and basically brushed us off. After a few minutes, Billy Ray was introduced to him, and the candidate put on this phony air and pretended to welcome him, all the while looking at me like I was a criminal.

As it turned out, he was elected and later convicted of some huge security fraud case and drummed out of office. His name was John Corzine, a candidate for governor of New Jersey, and the worst of all crooked politicians. I don't know for sure if Billy Ray was even feeling the same kind of vibe I was. I think he may have been so used to phony people that he was just another one to ignore.

After the Gore rally, management received a call from the Bush campaign and asked if Billy Ray could attend a rally at an airport hangar in Chattanooga. He accepted, and we loaded up on a bus and headed that way. When we got to the airport, there were thousands of people in the hangar, and Bush's plane was just touching down on the runway. When he was escorted into the hangar, "We The People" blared on the PA and the crowd was more than exuberant. Now, those folks seemed to be real people to me, unlike the two Democratic events I'd attended. Bush fired the crowd up, and Billy Ray ate it up.

Billy Ray and I had talked about whom he was going to vote for the following Tuesday, and although he never actually said, I have a feeling his dad may not have been so happy about his choice.

Nine years later, Cyrus was asked to headline a handful of concerts called the Sean Hannity Freedom Tour, featuring Michael W. Smith, Lee Greenwood, and Charlie Daniels. We did two shows a week for four weeks. Billy Ray had a ball, but didn't realize these were actually Republican rallies. He just didn't pay a lot of attention to correspondence from management, but he signed off on it, so it was a little too late once we were out there.

It was a fun tour, though. We always played cornhole pretty much everywhere we went and also liked to throw a football around. We were out in the parking lot on the first afternoon of the tour when Sean Hannity and Oliver North came over where we were and wanted to throw the ball with us. Jon Voight was also on the tour, and we got to bend his ear about many different subjects, including questions about his beautiful daughter, Angelina Jolie.

There were a ton of other celebrities out showing their support for Sean's cause. Mark Levin, the radio talk show host, gave me one of his books and signed it for me. Jim Caviezel, the actor who played Jesus in *The Passion of the Christ* was there; he was friendly and very soft-spoken. He and Billy Ray spent some time talking on Billy Ray's bus while I waited outside.

As I was standing there, a film crew came up, and Ainsley Earhardt, the Fox News anchor, asked if she could interview Mr. Cyrus.

I said, "Of course, but he's talking with Jesus right now." She laughed and said she could wait, but would love to interview me while she waited. I don't even remember what she asked me . . . something about the tour, I'm sure.

I met several Fox News personalities, including ultra-liberal Bob Beckel. He was a lot of fun that night in San Diego, but I can honestly say I can't go along with any of his views. He is OUT THERE!

The tour went very well, and Billy Ray finally realized he was sleeping with the enemy about the time it was over. Perfect timing. He was cool with it, though. Billy Ray is the most laid-back person I've ever worked with in the music business, and a fine man, to boot.

———

One of the pet peeves of most tour managers is the booking agency sending dates that are going to be nearly impossible to cover the distance overnight. One such instance was booked by our friend Steve Lassiter, or as music industry folks knew him, Sput. He had booked us in a place called Norway House, Manitoba.

I questioned him on how in the world we could make it there on time to do the show. It was 283 miles north of Winnipeg on the other side of Lake Winnipeg. There were no major highways, and the only flights going into Norway House were puddle jumpers.

Sput told me he had confidence that I would be able to pull it off, so he would be making the trip with us. We flew from Nashville to Winnipeg, and upon arrival, after securing our baggage from the commercial flight, we headed to the private terminal. When we got out on the tarmac to go to the plane, we were met by the pilots of the twin-engine plane, and they began asking everyone their weight and how much the equipment weighed, and so on. I asked them if there was a problem with the number of people we had, and the pilot said there was no problem. He was just trying to determine how much fuel to put in the plane. I said, "Heck, that's easy. Just fill that bad boy up." I was only half joking, but the other half was dead serious.

Well, we got off the ground, packed like sardines in this fuselage that was about the size of a short school bus. The flight was uneventful, but the fun started when we were banking to land on just the other side of this huge lake. I could see the runway, and it looked peculiar from the air. Its color was not the usual concrete or asphalt color, and when we touched down, I realized why. I heard rocks hitting the fuselage. It was a gravel runway, and this was a first for all of us.

We got in the vans and drove a short distance to a fairly nice hotel in the middle of an Indian reservation. Right across the street was the venue, and there were people lined up around the corner waiting for the show. We went over and did a sound check, and I got to talking to some of the locals. I was told that most of the people attending the show would come from fifty to one hundred miles away and that most of them would come by *canoe*. I was astounded that anyone in the world still lived like that, and that anyone having the choice would make that trip to see any artist. As it turned out, the show went well, and we left within a couple of hours to go back to the plane and fly back to a Winnipeg airport hotel.

The last surprise of the night came when we were preparing to take off from that same gravel runway, and a pickup truck hauled ass in front of us to scare the caribou and moose off the runway. It was, after all was said and done, a trip of a lifetime. In other words, I don't ever want to do that again in my life. Sput was proud of me for pulling it off, and we did get to see the Northern Lights from the plane on the way back to Winnipeg.

⸺⸱⸻

Another test came when I planned a two-day run from Nashville to

Wisconsin, where we did an afternoon show, flew on to Winnipeg, stayed overnight, and then did another festival the next afternoon, opening for George Strait. I got to meet him when Billy Ray went in to say hi, and was impressed with his graciousness. After that show, we reboarded our plane, and headed back to Nashville, stopping in Fargo, North Dakota, to clear customs. And oh yeah . . . this time the plane was not a puddle jumper. It was an Embraer Legacy corporate jet, and it was brand spanking new. It seated thirteen and it was just perfect for our band and crew. It cost Billy Ray forty grand for the two-day adventure, but we would have never made it any other way.

Billy Ray loved flying private jets, so he didn't mind that he made considerably less for that two-day run. He and I shared many jets during my time with him. We also flew in a couple of helicopters. One into Pocono Speedway in Pennsylvania, and the other with Mr. Mel Larsen, a good friend of Bruton Smith, the owner of several race tracks. We were picked up at the hotel and driven to Mr. Larsen's house on the outskirts of Las Vegas. We got in his Bell Jet Ranger helicopter, flew over Hoover Dam, then back into Vegas, landing inside Las Vegas Motor Speedway. We got in race cars in the passenger seats and took three hot laps around the track, got back in the helicopter, and flew straight down the Vegas Strip and back to Mr. Larsen's house. All this up-and-down stuff and the g-forces in the race car left me a little queasy. So, what did I do? I let Billy Ray talk me into riding the roller coaster. Well, that sent me over the edge.

All in all, it was a fun day in Vegas, except for the roller-coaster ending. Once I finally felt better, I loaded myself on the bus for a trip back across the country to the other Vegas: Nashvegas!

A "Bucket List" Gig

October 2001

A fter getting back home and recuperating from asphalt lag, I got a call from Al Schiltz, Billy Ray's manager. He asked me if I knew a bus driver who would like to drive to Alaska.

I asked him what the gig was, and he told me, "No gig." There was a man in Nashville who had terminal brain cancer, and he wanted to travel there so his wife and young stepson could see the Aurora Borealis, the Northern Lights. It was a bucket-list gig.

I asked Al how they planned to pay for the diesel fuel for a 45-foot tour bus. He mentioned that there had been a fund-raiser for the family, and they had collected what they hoped would be enough to make the trip. I told Al I would ask around, and when I mentioned it to a couple of my bus-driving buddies, it was the consensus that the trip would take a large portion of the money collected just for the fuel. I asked if there might be another way to pull it off. A car dealer in Murfreesboro, Tennessee, stepped up to the plate and offered a roomy van to make the trip. At that point, I did what I thought might be the family's best option: I volunteered to drive them myself. It was an adventure I had always wanted to take, and I figured I would never have another chance to make such a trip.

I picked up the van in Murfreesboro and headed over to the Kevin Royster family home to meet them for the first time, and to pack the van for an early departure the next morning. Helen, Kevin's wife, was a sweet lady, and she expressed to me her appreciation for volunteering to drive them on this epic journey. At that point, Kevin was still capable of walking, but he tired very easily, obviously, so we loaded up a wheelchair, just in case.

The next morning, we gathered up last-minute items and prepared to shove off. Helen, like me, enjoyed indulging in a little pot for relaxation, and she showed me her dugout that she planned to take with her. I told her that probably wouldn't be a good idea since we had to cross the Canadian border, going and coming. Then, I showed her what I planned to carry—just enough to get us to the Canadian border. After that, we would have to find something else for relaxation, like maybe some good wine. She agreed that was a good idea, and off we went. Our first stop was Branson, Missouri, where Helen's uncle had written a religious play that was showing. They were picked up at the hotel and taken to the play, and I decided to play golf on a course I'd played before when passing through Branson. We stayed there an extra day so they could visit with family and for Kevin to rest up before we started on our trip in earnest.

We headed north toward Sioux Falls, South Dakota—our destination for that day's travel. We arrived a little after dark, got rooms, had dinner, and Helen and I planned the next day's trip. Helen's mother had mapped out a route on MapQuest, and our next day was to take us through Winnipeg and across Manitoba into Edmonton, Alberta, and from there into British Columbia, where we would hit the Alaska Highway. I mentioned to Helen that might be the shortest route, but if Kevin was up for it, we could head west through Rapid City, South Dakota, and visit Mount Rushmore and the Crazy Horse monument.

She asked Kevin, who agreed, and so we did just that. Helen happened to have a friend who lived in Rapid City, so she called her, only to discover that she was out of town; however, the friend said we were more than welcome to stay in her house for a couple of days. We took her up on the generous offer. Kevin was pleased as punch that he and his little family got to see this fabulous part of America.

From there, we headed farther west into Wyoming and up through Montana, and the views were awe-inspiring. Mountain ranges with fresh snow covering the peaks and valleys filled with horses and cattle, antelope, and elk. We stayed in Billings one night, and from there, we headed toward Great Falls.

When we reached the Canadian border, a customs agent came over to the van and asked us a few questions about who we were and where we were going, if we had any weapons or contraband, and had we heard the news that the US Air Force had begun bombing Afghanistan thirty minutes earlier. Wow, that last part brought it all back home. Here we were, three weeks after 9/11, crossing over into Canada and wondering what in the world was going to happen to our country. As we drove into Canada, we were amazed at the number of American flags flying in a show of support for the USA.

That night, we stayed in Banff, Alberta. We had a wonderful meal at the hotel and retired for the night. About two a.m., I awoke to a frantic knock at the door. It was Helen telling me that Kevin had fallen in the bathroom and couldn't get off the floor. I followed her back to the room and helped Kevin up and back into his bed.

It was a long, sleepless night after that, so we decided to stay another night in Banff. The morning we were preparing to leave, Helen called me and asked if I could bring the wheelchair to her room. She suspected Kevin had suffered a stroke—he couldn't walk. With that news, I walked into their room and asked Kevin if he wanted to turn back and go home to Tennessee.

He shook his head and pointed north, and away we went. We

continued into the majestic Canadian Rockies to the small town of Prince George, British Columbia, and from there, we headed north to Dawson Creek and Mile Marker 0 of the Alaska Highway. I had heard the Alaska Highway had spots that were nearly impassable, but that was the route we wanted to go, so we dove right in. Along the way, there were places where the blacktop turned to gravel, but hardly impassable.

After eight hours of driving, we reached an oil boomtown called Fort Nelson. It was a neat little town and had all the conveniences, so we settled in for the next two nights in a local hotel. Kevin's condition didn't change from that point on, but we continued at his insistence. We were on a mission.

We spent the next night in Watson Lake, Yukon Territory, where the main tourist attraction was the Northern Lights Centre, which featured detail on how the Aurora Borealis happens.

On the remaining leg of the journey, we followed the Yukon River as it wound its way toward Alaska. We saw caribou, moose, and bald eagles in that natural paradise in the great Northwest. It was probably my favorite part of the trip. We stayed a night in Whitehorse, Yukon Territory, but Kevin's health was dwindling.

We had to get back home before things got much worse, so we opted not to go the additional miles to Juneau and would start back home the next day.

The first day on the return trip, I drove all the way from Whitehorse to Fort Nelson, a trip of six hundred-plus miles. The whole way back I was freaking out a little, wondering if we would be able to get gas. I would see cars with gas cans strapped to the roof, and this really scared me. Luckily, we found one gas station close to Watson Lake, filled up, and made it all the way to Fort Nelson. We saw the Northern Lights that night on the road, and it was magnificent, as always.

When we reached Fort Nelson late that night, Kevin had taken a turn for the worse. The long trip had done him in, and Helen wasn't sure if he could go any farther. She felt like they needed to fly home, but was worried about me driving alone all those miles. I assured her I would be okay and that we would do whatever we had to do.

The next morning, I told Helen I needed to get the oil changed, and we could see how Kevin felt before we got back on the road. While I was in the oil-change bay, the radio was playing, of all things, "Sweet Home Alabama." I couldn't resist. There were a crew of young guys, so I went out on a limb.

I said, "Hey, guys. Y'all probably won't believe this, but the band playing on the radio . . . well, I used to work for them."

They seemed impressed, so the next thing out of my mouth was, "I need some weed."

This one kid asked me, "How much?"

I told him just enough to get us back to the States. I figured three days at a couple of joints a day would get us there.

He said, "I'll be right back," and he was, with a quarter ounce of what is known to folks "in the know" as BC Bud. Bright green with reddish orange hairs. Scary looking. He charged me a hundred Canadian dollars, which was about sixty US dollars at the time. I was pleased.

When I got back to the hotel, Helen was sitting on the curb with her head in her hands. She was a basket case. I told her to come with me for a minute, and she jumped in the van with me, and we proceeded to partake.

When we got back to the hotel, her outlook had changed. She was smiling and told me she was going to give Kevin a little pot to see if it would help him.

I took the opportunity to take a drive out of town to a provincial park just to kill a little time. It was ten miles or so down a gravel road that turned into dirt and deposited me by this gorgeous lake with picnic tables on one side, backed up to a thick forest on the other side. It was deafeningly quiet. All I heard was the mournful call of a loon from the other side of the lake.

Suddenly, I heard a loud rustling in the forest behind me, and it made the hair on the back of my neck stand up. I decided I would leave this tranquility behind and head back to the hotel. I didn't know what the noise was, and I was surely not going to hang around to find out.

Eventually, after we'd arrived back to Tennessee, I Googled "provincial park, Fort Nelson, BC," and the first thing that popped up was a Sasquatch sighting near Fort Nelson. My luck, it was probably a grizzly. Either way, I was outta there.

When I got back to the hotel, Helen told me Kevin was feeling much better, and we should get some miles behind us.

Before we left, I decided that we had too much weed, so I drove back to the oil change place and returned half of what the young man had sold me. I explained we would have to throw it away when we got close to the border. He asked me if I wanted some of the money back, to which I said, "Heck no. We appreciate what you did for us."

We departed Fort Nelson and headed south for another two days. We reached the Canada/US border, making sure we had no weed left in the vehicle, knowing full well they would probably want to go through it extensively. We pulled up to the guard station where the lady officer asked for our IDs, asked if we had enjoyed our stay in Canada, and sent us on our way. That was it. Nothing more.

Our route on the way back to Tennessee took us through my old stomping grounds in Colorado, where we spent a couple of days. The Roysters stayed at a hotel, and I hightailed it to Freddie's place out in the mountains. As I have already mentioned, I would take any opportunity to visit with my old friend, and that was exactly what I did. He supplied me with enough pot to get us back home. The trip to Tennessee was uneventful but enjoyable, thanks to Freddie.

We got to Nashville, unloaded the van, and returned it to the car dealer. I had made some new friends very happy at a most unhappy time in their lives. I had provided Kevin a check mark on his bucket list, and I felt pretty good about that.

Kevin lived two more weeks after our return. His funeral was sad, but everyone there thanked me for doing what I had done for Kevin and his family. It was one of the most fulfilling things I have done in my life, and I am proud to have had the opportunity. Rest in Peace, Kevin.

TOUR BUS BLUES

When I first came on board with Cyrus, I recall sitting in catering, overhearing two bus drivers talking. One said, "How are those Cyrus boys to work with?" The other one laughed and said, "They're a bunch of good ole boys, but they sure smoke a lot of weed."

I laughed out loud and said, "It's a damn heap better than if they were drinking whiskey all day. I've worked with both kinds and I'll take the weed any day of the week."

We had our moments with it, though. We had just finished a show on an Indian reservation in the Upper Peninsula of Michigan, and most of us were waiting in the back lounge of the bus for the load-out to be complete. The diesel engines fired up, and we took it as our signal to do the same. We rolled out of the parking lot, and rode for about five minutes, and the intercom rings. I picked up the phone and it was Connie, our female driver. "Paul. There's a cop behind us." And in her next breath, "They're pulling us over."

Well, instantaneously, panic mode set in. Air freshener couldn't get all that smell out of the back lounge, and we couldn't open the windows because the cops were, by that time, standing by the front door. Connie said, "They want to talk to you."

I told the guys to find somewhere to hide all that stuff, which between us, was probably enough to bring charges. It was an ugly scene. If the police had infrared cameras, they would have seen about ten guys running into each other, trying to figure out what they were going to do with the weed. The two guys on the bus who didn't partake were not at all happy about our immediate circumstances.

I walked off the bus, and there were two big strapping Native American law-enforcement officers waiting for me. I asked them, very politely, "Can I help you guys?" Well, the good cop/bad cop scenario began. One officer said, "Our security cameras caught a big fellow sitting in the front lounge, and he was rolling something from a small bag. We need to talk to him. We aren't going to arrest him, but we want what he was rolling. All of it. And if he won't give it up, we'll call the canine unit and run the dogs through the bus."

I asked them to describe him to me, and to a tee, they described one of our guitar players. I got back on the bus, and Connie informed me we had just crossed over the reservation limit sign. This was good info, because I figured they were just going to hassle us a little and then let us go. Well, the perp agreed to give them what he had, and he walked off the bus and did as they asked. They gave him a good talking to, because he was out there fifteen minutes. When he got back on the bus, he told me the officers wanted to talk to me again. I was thinking, *Uh-oh. Not good.*

I asked the guys what they had done with all the stuff, and they pointed to the bathroom. I walked in there, opened the lid, and peered down through the baseball-sized hole in the bottom. It was full of weed bags, pipes, roach clips, and various and sundry paraphernalia. I walked back off the bus, and the good cop told me that we could go, but he wanted to walk through the bus first. I agreed to let him. I figured saying anything about a search warrant might bring out his bad side.

He walked onto the bus and was surprised to see a lady bus driver behind the wheel, which I will say right now was one of the best drivers I've ever slept behind. The officer came into the front lounge, greeted everybody, and continued walking right through the bunk area, where a couple of the smarter guys pretended they were sleeping with their curtains pulled. He walked into the back lounge, turned around, and headed through the front lounge and off the bus. He told Connie she could go; so, very cautiously, we got back on the road.

When we got to Traverse City, Michigan, we pulled into a service station and, literally right behind us was a state trooper. We stopped at the fuel pumps, and he walked over and asked me who we were and where had we played that night. I told him we worked for Billy Ray Cyrus and the name of the casino. He said, "I hope all went well, and that y'all had a good time." Well, he didn't actually say "y'all." I mean, he was a Michigander, after all. I said something to the effect of, "Yep, it was awesome, and our next stop is Nashville and home for a few days." He wished us safe travels, went in the store for a minute, and then drove off.

Feeling like we had dodged a second bullet, we got back on the bus and didn't get off again until we got to Nashville. Poor Connie had to keep a watch in her rearview mirror the whole way. Our old buddy Rogco, during the night, took it upon himself to take the toilet off its pedestal and retrieve all the weed, etc. By that time it had been peed on, and the blue liquid that is popular on buses had pretty much soaked it all. It was a total loss, but a lesson well-learned. *Never ever take more pot with you than you can eat.*

I called Billy Ray the next day to tell him what had happened and find out how he wanted me to handle it with Al Schiltz, the manager. He said not to tell him anything. The ol' *what he don't know won't hurt him.* I agreed with him wholeheartedly, but somehow, Al found out anyway. I never really knew for sure, but I guess he considered it a "no harm, no foul" situation. It was a night to remember . . . because it could never be forgotten.

Sly Dog and Skynyrd

I f everybody in the Billy Ray Cyrus organization had one thing in common, it was their love for Skynyrd music. I shared that same love for the music, but after ten years on the road and being discarded so abruptly, I really could care less if I saw any of them again. When we ended up on the same bill with them in Fort Loramie, Ohio, all the guys were excited about seeing and hearing them. I certainly could have cared less, but I did look forward to making a few of them feel uncomfortable.

We pulled up to the venue, and Skynyrd's buses were already there, so I eased on over and knocked on the door of one of the buses. Craig Reed came to the door, and I went on the bus and visited with Billy and Leon for a little while. Craig asked me if I wanted to see Johnny, Dale, and Gary on the other bus. I looked over Craig's shoulder at their bus, and I saw all three of them peeking out the windows, and when they saw me looking, they hid their faces. I told Craig no thanks, that I'd just seen all of them, and the fact that they knew I was there was plenty enough for me.

We did our set and, naturally, my guys wanted to stay and hear Skynyrd. They mentioned there was a balcony at stage left and we could watch from there. They wanted me to go along, so, reluctantly, I accompanied them to the balcony. I saw Gary glance over at us a few songs in, and he called Craig over by his amp and told him to tell us we couldn't stay there and watch the show. It was fine by me, but that day, he pissed off some big fans. And from that day on, no Skynyrd music was allowed on the bus and the name should never be spoken again. I told the guys not to let it get to them too much because Gary Rossington had done worse to people he called his friends.

It's funny that a few short years earlier, my wife and I were guests in his home numerous times. Well, our truck driver, Big Jeff, said it best when his Skynyrd cap blew off his head into the highway. When asked if he wanted to turn around and go get it, his answer was, "F--- Lynyrd Skynyrd."

And you know, after that day, I no longer held a grudge against any of them. I was damn happy to be where I was . . . with a bunch of the best friends I have ever had. Sly Dog.

DAVE MOODY

Corky Holbrook, Billy Ray's bass player, decided he was ready to give the road up. He had been talking about it and finally acted on it. Billy Ray's brother, Mick Adkins, had a friend who lived in Louisville, Kentucky. Mick claimed this guy was one hell of a bass player and would fit right in with all the rest of us. Of course, we were all wary about anybody Mick might recommend. It was imperative for a guitarist to play well, yes; but he also had to be able to get along with eleven other guys while rolling down the highway in a forty-five-foot tube.

The music part was no problem at all for Dave Moody, but the road part took a lot of getting used to. Dave had never really traveled on a tour bus, and there were a lot of little things that had to be adhered to so everyone stayed happy. Well, we hazed Dave pretty good. He was bad about leaving his bag and an old, black, Bret Michaels-type straw hat lying around in the front lounge, and when you are traveling with that many people, seating space is at a premium. We were sitting at a truck stop along I-40 in windy Oklahoma. I had called ahead and ordered us a bunch of pizzas to pick up while we refueled. Dave's ugly old hat was on the front lounge table, and I was sitting there, feeling a little mischievous. So, I picked up the hat, and told Dave, "This is what we're going to do with stuff that is left lying around." I then opened the window and tossed it out. While everybody was laughing, I could tell Dave was a little PO'd. I got up to walk off the bus and get his hat, but when I looked out the opposite window, I saw his hat blow out onto the driveway of the truck stop. An eighteen-wheeler ran right over it, flattened it. Then a burst of wind blew it out into the road, and away it went forever. I felt bad for a minute. Or less.

We always gave Dave hell, but he was a good sport. Especially the time all of us went to a luau in Hawaii. Wives and girlfriends in attendance, Dave donned the grass skirt and coconut bra to the delight of everyone there. We laughed so hard, it hurt. It was an awesome week on Waikiki for all of us. We all gathered down on the beach daily and just enjoyed each other's company. We were in Hawaii for six days and then played a show on the Fourth of July. Billy Ray chartered in, did the show, and chartered out. So we took his suite at the hotel overlooking the ocean and had a great party. The hotel even allowed us to spend his room service comp—three hundred bucks. Having a boss who doesn't hang around long has its benefits.

Now anyone who knows Dave Moody is aware that he is one of the most ardent Pittsburgh Steelers fans known to man. Totally unexpected, I got a contract from management that I needed to advance a one-hour fan appreciation concert in the parking lot of the Steelers stadium. When I told Dave about it, he almost came unglued. He was ecstatic. When we pulled up that morning, we were shown to our dressing room, and on the way to the stadium, we had to walk through the Steelers locker room. Our team contact took Dave up to meet Dan Rooney, the team owner. He offered Dave a Terry Bradshaw-autographed football. Dave had Mr. Rooney sign the ball as well, creating a one-of-a-kind collectible. He also came back with dozens of caps and t-shirts for all of us.

Dave was so proud of that ball. He bragged about it all the way to our next stop. When he went to bed, he was in Steeler heaven. When he woke up, he was in reality hell. During the night, Steve French, a.k.a. Tito Frenchie, had a few too many Miller Lites and was admiring the football, and somehow, he ended up with a Sharpie in his hand. And the devil made him add another signature on the ball: Tito Frenchie. *Oh my God!* Dave was fit to be tied, but he never showed any anger toward Steve.

I'm not sure if Dave ever "fixed" the ball. If nothing else, he has a great story to tell. By the way, Dave kept up his relationship with the Steelers front office and his band Jefferson Tarc Bus plays at several Steeler events during the season. Pretty cool stuff. He also has an AC/DC tribute band called Thunderstruck and they are doing quite well around the country.

"THERE'S MY BUS!"

illy Ray Cyrus and Sly Dog were playing an early show at a large nightclub just outside the grounds of the Star Lake Amphitheater in Pittsburgh. Before the show started, Billy Ray came to me and asked me to see if he and I could go next door to the amphitheater after the show and see Stevie Nicks and Sheryl Crow. That was always an easy thing for me to arrange, and I had it done in a matter of a phone call. After the show, I hustled him out of the club into a car and over to the backstage entrance of the amphitheater. We were met by security and escorted to a couple of seats near the front of house soundboard. They were both onstage and singing my favorite Stevie Nicks song, "Landslide," and they knocked it out of the park. The show ended a few songs later, and we were escorted backstage to meet Sheryl and Stevie.

There was no one else there; we had them all to ourselves. They hadn't planned a meet-and-greet after the show, but they made special concessions for Billy Ray.

Billy Ray started talking about the PBR (the Professional Bull Riders Association), because he had just recently recorded a song for a compilation album he had done for them. I was wondering where he was going with this, and he asked Sheryl, "Hey, isn't your boyfriend a bull rider?"

Sheryl look a little perplexed and answered, "That's Jewel!"

Well, Billy Ray apologized to Sheryl, and we all had a good laugh, with Sheryl laughing the loudest. Then he said to me,

"Paul, I think my bus driver is ready to roll," and with hurried goodbyes, away we went. The guys in Sly Dog will all tell you that whenever Billy Ray was feeling a little uncomfortable, he would say, "There's my bus!" and he'd be gone. He and I laughed about it on the ride back over to the buses. I shared some great times with Billy Ray, and this was certainly one of them.

Anyway, Sheryl probably didn't hold it against him. She later accepted an invitation to be in the all-star band that played at the Country Music Hall of Fame after the world premiere of *Hannah Montana: The Movie*.

MILEY'S METEORIC RISE TO FAME

I first met Miley when she was around the age of five. We were doing a show at Dollywood in Pigeon Forge, Tennessee, and Tish had brought Miley and her brother to see her dad's show. Miley would come out at that early age and get center stage and sing with her father. Miley is the goddaughter of Dolly Parton, so it stands to reason she would be a star. Even back then, her pitch was excellent, and I had a feeling she was gonna move into the business at some point. I never knew how much so until seven or eight years later when she landed the role of Hannah Montana, and Billy Ray went along to play her father in the highly rated Disney TV show. After getting to know Miley, she and I invented a secret handshake, which we'd always use whenever we would see each other.

One other time, a few years later after Miley had become Hannah, my coworker Greg Hagewood and I went to Toluca Lake, California, to do some work for the Cyruses at the house. They also owned a condo a few blocks from their home, and that was where we stayed, along with Miley's boyfriend Justin Gaston, a competitor on *Nashville Star*. Greg and I were given free rein with our Cyrus credit cards to get what we needed at the store for the condo. We did the usual bachelor stuff, like cookies and candy and microwave popcorn. We also had free rein to use the cards to go out and eat every night, so we pretty much did. Great Mexican restaurants and breakfast places in Hollywood. We made the rounds, and people began to recognize Greg and me together. The paparazzi hanging out down the street would stop us and ask if Miley was home. Usually she wasn't, but we would always say she was, just to keep them hanging on.

⸺⸻⸺

Greg and I did a lot of work for them in Cali. We pulled up the big flagstone slabs that the previous owner had put down, and we built patios with pavers. We spent many an hour and many a dollar at Lowe's.

Miley had bought her first car, a Porsche Cayenne, the SUV, and when she was learning to maneuver her driveway, she nearly pulled the bumper off against a palm tree. After that, she wouldn't drive it anymore, so Greg and I used it as a RUV, a *real* utility vehicle. We would leave Lowe's with lumber sticking out the back hatch and would get some crazy looks. Heck, *whatever works* is my motto. We even went from Toluca Lake to Brandi Cyrus's apartment to help her move. We strapped a mattress and box springs to the top of Miley's car. Man, you talk about the Beverly Hillbillies. We probably caused wrecks coming back across Hollywood.

⸺⸻⸺

Greg and I became fast friends and still are. We got a lot of funny looks from people. We joked they may have thought we were gay, but hell, we were in California, and most all of them were gay.

On another trip, Greg and I drove from Tennessee to Toluca Lake, literally over New Year's. We stopped several times along the way to do some sightseeing, but our mission was to deliver a sweet dog that had been left at the farm, and Billy Ray wanted her in California. We stopped for dinner one night, and the server was a sweet girl. She asked us about our accents and where we were heading. Well, I couldn't resist. I told her we were from Tennessee, and we were on the way to California to get married, because they don't play that stuff in Tennessee. Her eyes were wide as saucers, and poor old Greg almost fell out of his chair. After a little bit, I let her know I was only kidding, because I'm a smartass. She laughed, and we left her a mighty fine tip . . . on Billy Ray's credit card, of course.

<hr>

After a few weeks of work, we needed to get back to Tennessee to see about Singin' Hills, Billy Ray's 600-acre spread in Thompson's Station, about thirty miles south of Nashville. This farm was like heaven on earth. There was no one there most of the time, although we did have to contend with Billy Ray's brother Mick and his mother Ruthie Adkins occasionally. They lived right down the road, and Ruthie was great, but Mick loved to keep it stirred up. I never was sure what his problem was with me, but I am positive he did not like me one bit. I can't think of many people in this world who actually don't like me, but this hillbilly hated me and made it very hard to work for Billy Ray. We stayed in Tennessee a few weeks, and then headed back to Cali. When we got to the condo, we looked in the cabinets and all our good stuff was gone. I saw Miley the next morning and I asked her if she and Justin had eaten all that candy and junk. She said her mother had thrown it all away. For the record, we did restock.

<hr>

While we were in Los Angeles that time, Miley brought home a demo of a song she wanted us to hear. She played it for us, and I was thinking: *This song is incredible. It could be huge.* Later, when her CD was released, the song rose to the top of the charts and was played constantly. It was called "The Climb" and had a prominent part in the Hannah Montana movie.

It was a surreal experience to talk with Miley after she had become a huge star. Billy Ray and Sly Dog were out doing shows and somehow we ended up in California right about the time Miley's tour hit Oakland. We rode the bus in from Yosemite Park and hung out backstage before the show. When Miley saw me, she came running over and gave me a great big hug, backed off, and said, "Secret handshake," and she remembered every move. I can't say that I did, but I made it through it. It had actually been several years since I had seen her last.

That night, I saw Miley in a whole different light. She had grown up onstage, and it was the most natural place for her to be. The production was incredible, and the cast was huge. Miley had broken through, and she was off and running . . . and for a while, the biggest star on the planet.

SEEING THE USA

T he members of Sly Dog, along with the crew, filled every bunk on the bus, all twelve. We were one big happy family, but we had our moments and we "sho nuf" had some fun. We had been in Branson, Missouri, for two days, and during the day, we usually went off in different directions; some went fishing and some played golf (me). Probably the most fun we ever had was at the go-cart track. It was a hoot. We all did some serious racing in the carts. The track was made out of wood slats, and it had a corkscrew turn that took you up to a higher level, then down and around other turns. Our merchandising guy, the world-famous Jim Carson, did some kind of deal with the guy who was running the place, and we rode for free over and over again. Anyway, we would fill the hours with fun stuff, and it made being away from our homes and families a whole lot easier.

With that in mind, I knew all the guys were not looking forward to going home for a day and a half and then getting back on the bus to go to Blackfoot, Idaho, to play the Blackfoot County Fair. I looked at a map, and the wheels in my head started turning. If we left from Branson and headed northwest toward Blackfoot, we could be in Jackson Hole in plenty of time to spend three days in the area. The Grand Tetons and Yellowstone were waiting. I called a small hotel in Jackson, and since tourist season ended on Labor Day, they had plenty of room for us; however, in order to save money, I snagged a few rooms for cleaning up, but almost everybody would sleep on the bus in the parking lot.

My next move was to go to the guys and see if they were all game to do it. Duh! They jumped at the idea. Next, I went to Billy Ray and told him what we planned on doing, and he said, "As long as you're there to pick me up at the Idaho airport, I don't care what you guys do. And while you're there in Jackson Hole, treat them all to a dinner on the corporate AMEX card." Now those were the kind of orders I liked to take from a boss. Billy Ray was a good one, for sure.

With Billy Ray's approval already in hand, I called Al Schiltz, the manager, just to tell him what our plans were and to assure him that it wasn't going to be a costly venture. I had already saved them a thousand dollars in fuel by not going back to Nashville and heading straight out to Wyoming.

When we got to Jackson, we rented a couple of vans and convoyed up into Yellowstone and did the sightseeing thing: Old Faithful, the Thermal Pools, Grand Canyon of the Yellowstone River, and Lamar Valley. We spent the entire first day in Yellowstone, driving out after dark. This was the day Jim Carson made us turn the convoy around because he'd seen an elk. We got back up there, and there was a little mule deer, of which we had already seen a thousand. Carson said, "It was an elk in a deer suit." He never lived it down, but I'm here to say right now that Jimmy Carson will make you laugh so hard, you will wet your pants. Everybody in the music business who knows him loves him.

The next day we went through Teton National Park and spent a lot of the day in Jackson. Lots to see and do. Then out on the Elk Refuge to the Gros Ventre Mountains. Some of the most majestic views on the planet. We found some great places to eat like Bubba's Barbeque, and I took the guys to dinner on Billy Ray at the Gun Barrel, a fine establishment that serves game dishes like elk, antelope, and bison. Incredible meal.

CROWDS...OR NOT

D uring the time I toured with Billy Ray and Sly Dog, we got to see a number of National Parks along the way. We saw Rocky Mountain National Park, Glacier, Yellowstone, Tetons, Yosemite, Sequoia, King's Canyon, and Redwoods. We spent days off in Los Angeles, Phoenix, and New York City— from the Atlantic to the Pacific. We played shows in every venue imaginable from coast to coast, and in Canada and Mexico. We played in ballparks, small and large auditoriums, stadiums, and a hundred Indian casinos.

We had great crowds almost everywhere we went, though there were some that went the other way. Tuba City, Arizona, on a Navajo reservation, was just such a day. The whole day had seemed a little weird from the time we drove up. That little "town" had empty streets. Nobody to be seen other than right there where the show was. It was in a community center right smack in the middle of everything. And if someone can tell me what tying tennis shoes together and throwing them over the power lines means, I would appreciate it.

Anyway, Billy Ray flew in on a private jet, but he had to land in Flagstaff. The whole day, nobody knew where the promoter was, and I wasn't going to let anybody take anything off the truck until I got the $75,000 check. He finally showed up and told me he had made an enormous mistake and had booked the date on the same day as the Gathering of Nations in Albuquerque. I said that we are here ready to do the show and I must have the payment before we go any further. He reluctantly handed me the check, and we loaded in, sound checked, and ate before Billy Ray showed up. When he got there, I told him we would probably have a small crowd that night, though we had been paid. We did a complete show to the *six people* who did not go to Albuquerque. It was ugly. The promoter kept asking me for a reduction, and I told him that certainly wasn't up to me. Well, he wanted to talk to Billy Ray about it, and I wouldn't let him near him. His beef was with the booking agent in Nashville and his dumb self.

When the show was over, Billy Ray asked me if I wanted to fly back to Nashville with him on the Lear. Corky Holbrook and I loaded up for the long drive to Flagstaff and then the flight to Nashville. The rest of the guys loaded up on the bus. I know the rest of the guys probably had a few choice things to say about me and Corky, but the flight was beautiful. There was a line of thunderstorms way down below us, all the way across the country. We got to Nashville, got my truck, and I drove Billy Ray home to Singin' Hills Farm in Thompson's Station. About the time I let him out, the rain that had been chasing us arrived, and it rained on me the next forty miles until I got home. Still better than the 1,600 miles on a bus. Sorry, guys!

THE WEST COAST RUN

One of the most memorable trips I took with Sly Dog was a West Coast run, and I literally mean West Coast. We played the House of Blues at Disneyland, and after the show, we piled on the bus and I told the driver we wanted to wake up in Eureka, California. Our final destination was Lincoln City, Oregon, at a casino right on the Pacific Ocean. We met a friend there who provided us with some of Humboldt County's finest, and we decided to stay in the area, since our show in Lincoln City was still days away.

We found a little motel in Garberville, California, and I rented several rooms for showering, and we slept on the bus. The first day, some of the guys wanted to visit a buddy's home, where he grew some fine bud. I opted to take one of the rental cars and drive to the coast.

I found a state park that was right down by the ocean, and honestly, it was a little disconcerting to me. I was there all alone, not another soul in sight. I started thinking about all the horror movies that had settings just like the place I was in. It was getting near sunset, so I stayed long enough to witness the gorgeous Pacific Coast sunset offering an incredibly colorful display with huge waves crashing against the shore.

I headed on back to Garberville and got there just in time to enjoy some pickin' and grinnin' in the front of the motel. The local police kept driving by and checking us out, but we figured since we were in Humboldt County, they wouldn't bother us . . . and they didn't.

After a couple of days, we headed on up the Pacific Coast Highway toward Oregon. We followed the historic highway all the way, and it was truly a wonderful trip, although it worked the heck out of the driver with all the twists and turns as it ran along the ocean. We checked into our rooms when we got there, and looking out the window, we were right on the ocean. I never slept so well as those two nights in Lincoln City.

THE LAST LONG RUN

The last long bus trip we took was a humdinger. We did a show in a Michigan casino, left there for a North Dakota casino, and left there for a festival in Washington. We stopped in Bozeman, Montana, for a day and planned to drive down to Yellowstone, but fires had the north gate closed, so we found things to do in Bozeman. We drove on to Yakima, Washington, and after the show, I gave the guys the option of flying home or taking the bus back across the country. Only John Griffiths opted to fly, so we dropped him off at the Salt Lake City Airport, and we stayed in Park City that day while our driver got some sleep.

That night, we traveled to Manitou Springs, Colorado, and rented a couple of cars. Well, it was a no-brainer for me. I asked some of the guys if they would like to go visit my buddy, Freddie. Carson, T-Bone, and Norris took me up on it, and we headed up Ute Pass to Freddie's place near Lake George. He was shocked and pleasantly surprised to see us, and it was a day well spent. Any day I could spend with Freddie was a good day.

It was an uneventful two-day trip home from Colorado. By this time of the journey, we were all pretty much burned out and ready to get off the bus, for good. Little did we know, this would be our last long run on the bus. Oh, what we would all give to get back on a bus as a group again.

More than a Band

While working with several artists and the respective bands and crews, hands down, Billy Ray Cyrus and Sly Dog were head and shoulders above the others.

Quick note: *Now don't get me wrong. I made some real good friends in Skynyrd's crew in the ten years I worked with them. Some were fun to be around and some were not. There were a bunch of good musicians in the crew, which sure made it nice when our hotel would be too far away to do a sound check. We were doing a gig at Red Rocks outside of Denver and since the venue was part of Red Rocks Park, it was open all day. Concertgoers could actually get in their seats in the morning if they wanted to. Around sound check time, the ninety-five hundred-plus seats were half-filled and we asked the band's crew, which was different from the road crew, to do a good sound check, and we would show up forty-five minutes before Skynyrd's set. When we arrived, the stage manager came running up, all excited, yelling, "The roadie band got a standing ovation!" I have to say, that was pretty cool.*

Sly Dog was actually all of us . . . band members and road crew alike, or at least that's the way we saw it, and I'm sure all the fans felt that way too. We were a tight-knit group. We would roll into town and get things done and have fun doing it. I was the newest member of the group. Everyone else had been with Billy Ray a long time, so when his tour manager kinda burned out, I stepped in and was amazed at how easygoing everyone was.

They had all heard that I had been with Skynyrd, and

there were a thousand questions, especially from Michael "Joe" Sagraves. M.J. played multiple instruments, electric and acoustic guitar, pedal steel guitar, and there was one song where he played the mandolin. The running joke was Michael Joe was my favorite of all the guys, but all the guys meant the world to me. Terry Shelton played lead guitar and was the band leader. He was a burly West Virginia hillbilly with a big booming voice, and a good friend. Terry and I were watching the Daytona 500 at his house when Dale Earnhardt was killed. Steve French, or Tito Frenchie, as we called him, was the drummer when he had to leave the road due to an illness. Billy Copeland was a roadie who played drums, so he filled in for Steve. When Steve came back, he got a set of electronic drums and Billy stayed on his drums. Steve was a wonderful singer and harmonizer so Billy Ray did the best thing for everyone concerned.

Barton Stevens was keyboardist/backing vocalist/computer geek and just a hair eccentric, but a helluva lot of fun to be around. Norris Sherrill was also a roadie, and when necessity called up, he joined the band. He played lead and rhythm guitar and backing vocalist.

When I first began working with Billy Ray Cyrus, Don Von Tress was on the road with us. He was the writer of the song that gave Billy Ray his start, "Achy Breaky Heart." I always enjoyed Don, but he left the road abruptly, and although I have talked with him, I haven't seen him again since.

My golf buddy and bass player, Corky Holbrook was a character and a half. Great guy, but loved to complain. Every tour has one, but Corky was a great guy and had been around since the very beginning with Billy Ray. My most vivid memory of Corky was when he came in the back lounge complaining about something and T-bone threatened to "snap him like a twig." That's the closest we ever came to an altercation . . . so unlike the Skynyrd bunch. I think Corky quit shortly after that. After a couple of other bass players came and went, Dave Moody took over the bass position and fit in well. He did have a little of that AC/DC look, though. Not exactly a country look, but he got his parts.

———————

When Sly Dog had to fly, it was an ordeal, but some trips weren't possible in a bus, so we would meet at the Nashville airport. One instance, we were flying from Nashville to Seattle to do a couple of USO shows, one in Seattle and the other in Anchorage. While we were waiting at the gate, John Kay of Steppenwolf checked in to the same flight we were on. Now understand that a cross-country flight like this on Southwest Airlines was plenty long enough for my guys (and me) to get a good alcohol buzz. We always congregated at the back of the plane so we wouldn't bother any of the other passengers. To make it worse, flight attendants would hand us complete books of drink coupons. Still, we weren't nuisances or anything like that. We just tended to get a little loud, and hillbillies could be a little disruptive.

John Kay was in a row about ten up from where we were, and I noticed him turning around and looking at us, smiling at our antics. We may have been twenty minutes from Seattle, and just as if it were done on cue, we all started singing, "Get your motor runnin' . . ."

John Kay got up and came back where we were and said, "I know you guys have to be a band. Who do you work with?" We told him and he chuckled, "I knew it had to be some Nashville act."

I said, "I hope we didn't bother you. See, we were given all these drink coupons and didn't want them to go to waste."

He got a big laugh out of that and said, "Heck no. Everybody on this plane has enjoyed you guys today. I hope I have the good fortune to meet you all again." He was as friendly as any artist I had ever met, and I told him so. He said, "Just being me, my friend." What a great guy!

———

We had just finished a show in Connecticut, and we had recorded the Bristol night race to watch on the ride back to Nashville. The race was almost over; everybody except me decided to watch the end of the race. I was sitting in the jump seat by the driver as we rolled through New York City and on into New Jersey. All of a sudden, I hear all this whooping and hollering coming from the back lounge. The race was over and obviously had an exciting ending. All the guys had already been instructed not to tell me who won or how it ended, so before any of them could let it slip, I went to the back lounge and started the race from the beginning.

Anybody who has ever watched the Bristol race has seen how they "trade paint" throughout the entire race, and the drivers' wits as well as stamina are tested from start to finish. Dale Earnhardt had run out front a few times during the race and stayed pretty close to the top ten all the way. Seeing the Intimidator run this good always made me happy. So I watched as the race wound down, and the number 5 car looked like it had it in the bag. The laps go really fast at Bristol since it's only a half-mile track, and for Earnhardt, time was running out. Three laps to go, Earnhardt pulled up to Terry Labonte's back bumper and stayed right there through the next two laps. The white flag was out. One lap to go, and you couldn't put a postage stamp between the two bumpers. As Labonte came out of turn three, Earnhardt tapped his rear left bumper, and around the 5 car went. Earnhardt crossed the finish line in first place. Although Labonte was certainly pissed, all he said after the race was, "That's just racin'."

Earnhardt had said, "I didn't mean to spin Terry out. I just wanted to rattle his cage." Well, he sure did.

And then I knew what the guys were hootin' and hollerin' about earlier.

In early 2017, we found out our buddy, Jim Carson, had developed esophageal cancer and was given a year to live. We all made it a point to see him. A rather large get-together was planned at SoundCheck in Nashville for all of his friends in the music and merchandise business. It was a joyful occasion. Jim had lost a lot of weight, and though he looked good overall, there was no denying his illness. He had been treated with chemo for the past several months, and from all indications thus far, the tumor was shrinking.

We prayed daily for Jimmy Carson, and we all promised him we would gather next year at the same time for another get-together. I have a feeling he will defy the doctor's prognosis, and Jimmy will be there to greet us once again.

RICHARD CHILDRESS

Billy Ray and the band were performing on the TNN show *Prime Time Country* and on that same show was Richard Childress, Dale Earnhardt's car owner. I told him we had met when the Skynyrd guys came to Atlanta a few years back. He was a super nice guy and asked me if I could get his grandsons, Ty and Austin, Billy Ray Cyrus-autographed pictures. I did and when I handed them over, he said, "You ever need anything, you let me know."

Boy oh boy, he shouldn't have told me that.

We were booked to play for the Lexington, North Carolina, Barbeque Festival, which was a neighboring town to Welcome, the home of Richard Childress Racing. I contacted Richard, gave him our schedule, and asked if we could come by and tour the shop on the Saturday before Rockingham. He said, "No problem at all," and gave me the contact name and number of the gentleman who would show us around.

He then asked me "Are you going to the race tomorrow in Rockingham?" I said, "No, sir. We probably need to get on back to Nashville." He told me if we could come, he would set it up for us. I reminded him there were thirteen of us, including the driver. He said it was no problem and that I should give him a list of names and driver's license numbers, and to show up at the credentials office at the track and everything we would need would be there.

Now, y'all, this was a big deal for a man of his status to go out of his way for us, and we were all thinking that we would go there and nothing would be waiting for us.

We did the tour of Richard Childress Racing, including the R&D Department, the wind tunnel, and the three cars lined up in a shop with floors so clean, you could eat off them. Incredible access. We finished the shop tour and did the show. I sent Billy Ray on his way in his bus. Then we all loaded up with enormous anticipation and made our way to The Rock.

Our driver drove the eighty miles, parked the bus, and left it running, so we wouldn't wake up; when we did wake up, the credentials office was right outside the bus door. Unreal. And to top it off, all the paperwork was there. We were guests of Richard Childress and by default, Dale Earnhardt. It said so on the garage/pit passes he had left for all of us and a bus parking pass just outside the track, easy walking distance. We had the run of the place, and the guys had a day none of them will soon forget— including me, of course.

During some of my conversations with Chocolate Myers, he mentioned that Childress had a huge Christmas party every year and usually got a Nashville act to play for it. I hit him up, and he loved the idea, and so Sly Dog was hired to play for his Christmas party in 2001, sadly the same year that Earnhardt passed away. It was still a lot of fun. They had door prizes like ATVs, boats, and hunting trips. All the RCR drivers and crew members and their families were there. We were treated like a part of one big happy family that night. We didn't win a door prize, though . . . ha!

—————

My next encounter with Richard Childress was at the California Speedway for the spring race. Billy Ray was singing the anthem for the Saturday race, and he and I were asked to sit in on the drivers' meeting before the race began. It was pretty cool. There were several TV and movie stars, and a baseball hero of mine, Reggie Jackson, was there too. When the meeting was over, driver Morgan Shepherd came over to me and said, "Man, you look great. How did you lose the weight?"

I was more than a little puzzled, because I *had* lost weight, but how would Morgan Shepherd know that? I said, "Well, I just watched my portions and didn't try to eat everything in sight."

He said, "Well, you look great, Chocolate!"

I about fell out. I laughed and told him who I was, and that Chocolate often introduces me as his brother because we look so much alike. Morgan laughed and apologized. I got such a kick out of it, I went straight down to Jeff Burton's car hauler and searched out Richard Childress. I told him what happened, and he laughed his butt off and said, "Let's call Chocolate." He dialed him up and when Choc answered, Richard handed me his phone so I could tell Chocolate what had happened. Chocolate was at Lowe's with his wife Caron at the time, and when I told him, his laugh was echoing all over the building. I sure miss seeing my brother Chocolate and his bride, Caron. They graciously had me as a guest in their home. They are great folks and ardent ambassadors for NASCAR, and Chocolate is the most recognizable crew member ever.

SUPER FANS

The fans of Billy Ray Cyrus were way more than "die hard." I recall the very first day I was at the farm, I noticed this big white van sitting out by the fence near the school entrance. Sly Dog was rehearsing in the school, and I was about to meet them all for the first time. Michael Joe told me I needed to go out and meet the folks in that van, and that's basically all he said.

So, I went through the gate, and there in the van, for the very first time of many, I met Mrs. Polly Barfield and her daughter, Evelyn Wright. Her van was completely filled with pictures of Billy Ray and Sly Dog, and I quickly realized that was probably the biggest fan Billy Ray Cyrus ever had. She was a sweetheart, and I instantly fell in love with Polly and Evelyn.

Through the years, we would see them often—and it was always a pleasure. Polly was pretty well known by all the other fans, and I do believe, some of them were terribly jealous of her. I'll admit we might have given Polly and her crew a little more attention than the others at times, but . . . what can I say?

Once, when we were on the way to a gig in Florida, our trip took us right through Warner Robins, Georgia—Polly's hometown. She and I had prearranged for the band and crew to stop in for breakfast on the way. We arrived, and the spread was unbelievable. We spent an hour or so with them, and then headed on to Florida. It was an enjoyable visit, and it surely made Polly's highlight list.

A year or so later, Billy Ray and I jumped on the bus and headed for Atlanta Motor Speedway for the NAPA 500, where he'd been asked to sing the National Anthem before the race. Before we left, we'd learned that Polly was in the hospital in Atlanta—in a coma. When we finished up at the track, we went by the hospital to see her, although she might not know we were there. Evelyn told us later that she believed her mom knew, or at least, that's what we all chose to believe.

A week later, we were in Las Vegas and we got the news that Polly had passed away. Billy Ray dedicated "Some Gave All" to her that night. Polly was a great friend to all of us, and she was missed terribly from our shows after that.

Billy Ray's fan club was called the Spirit, and most of the members were ladies. He would meet-and-greet every night with at least thirty members, and more often than not, an additional thirty to forty people would attend. I became friends with most all of the fan club members through the years, and although I don't get to see them anymore, I stay in touch with quite a few of them via Facebook.

Passport Melee

Billy Ray, Regis and Kelly

The tour was over. My last duty was to book flights to Nassau, Bahamas, for Billy Ray and Sly Dog's appearance on *Live! with Regis and Kelly*, which was being televised from the Atlantis Resort. Management had negotiated the deal and decided I could do all the advance work and remain stateside. I was happy to do it. My plan was to ride down to Mississippi and visit my mother and brother Carl and his family. I always stayed with my longtime friend, Barry Burns, and his wife Helen in Wayside. It was always a hoot with them. We would laugh and reminisce about the good ole days when we spent all our spare time on the lake, drinking beer.

Then I got the call from Al Schiltz. Billy Ray had left his passport in his luggage that was on the way back to California on the tour bus, and I was to track it down and figure out how to get the passport to Billy Ray. He was able to get into the Bahamas, but he would need it to get back out. Now that was a challenge, and I stepped up. I tracked his driver down in Odessa, Texas. He found the passport exactly where Billy Ray had said it was.

Now, this was the fun part. I checked flight schedules out of Midland/Odessa Airport in Texas to Memphis and found one that would work, if the driver could get the passport there right away and talk the airlines into pulling some strings for us. It worked like a charm. He put the passport right in the hands of a Continental pilot who was going straight to Memphis via Houston and would be there the next morning at 8:00 a.m.

I left immediately and checked into an airport hotel in Memphis three hours later. I had a good room-service meal (on Billy Ray, of course) and was at the airport in plenty of time to meet the pilot. Fifteen minutes after the plane landed, the pilot hand-delivered the passport to me. I had already booked a flight out of Memphis to Nassau, and away I went. When I landed in Nassau, I cleared customs and headed toward the taxi stand. I hurriedly jumped in the front seat, always my preference, and we headed toward Atlantis through some of the most depressed areas I have ever seen—and remember, I'm from the Mississippi Delta, so I've seen bad neighborhoods. As we were rolling down the road, the driver said, "Just over there is the cemetery where Anna Nicole Smith is buried." I turned in my seat to look over my right shoulder, and sure enough, there was a small cemetery on a hill with only one prominent monument. Nice guy, the driver, so I asked him for his card so I could write a receipt for the cab fare.

We crossed a bridge, and sprawled out in front of me is Atlantis. I paid the cab driver, thanked him, and sent him on his way. I rang Billy Ray to let him know I was on the way up. In the elevator, I started looking for MY passport. I checked every pocket in my bag and in my pants . . . and no passport. I knocked on Billy Ray's room door, and when he opened the door, I said, "Here's your passport. Now I have to find mine." *Oh no!*

Yep. I couldn't imagine what I had done with it. I went up to Steve French's room to let them know I was there and to use his room phone to call the taxi driver. I had to leave a message, and my next call was to the American Embassy to let them know my situation. They weren't a lot of help. They said I would have to come down and fill out a lot of paperwork, and maybe in three days, the bureaucracy maybe would get me out of there. I was freaking out good about then. That is, until the driver's son called me and said his father had left his phone at home, but that he'd talked to him. The driver had found my passport on the front floorboard of his cab and promised to leave it at customs at the airport. I was still a lot concerned, but relieved a little. We had some lunch at a beach cafe near the hotel. We went back to the room and indulged in something the guys had picked up the night before at some locals club on the other side of the bridge. In other words, they took their lives and all their money in their hands to find some weed . . . oh, and some Cuban cigars. Crazy times, all in all, but in a little while, we were all in limos on the way to the airport. When I got there, I was met by a customs officer with my passport. What a relief! We had a few drinks in the bar, had a bunch of laughs like we always do, and then all boarded the flight to Atlanta.

In Atlanta, we all hit the skies, going in different directions, the West Virginia boys to the airport in Huntington, West Virginia, and the Middle Tennessee bunch to Nashville. Billy Ray flew on to Burbank. Me . . . I had to go back to Memphis and then back to Mississippi to finish my visit with my family.

GIFT FROM GIBSON

O n the flight to Memphis, a familiar face sat next to me, and we struck up a conversation. He asked what I did, and I proceeded to tell him about the above and beyond the call of duty I'd just undergone. I had met this man before, but he didn't remember me. He was Henry Juszkiewicz, the CEO of Gibson Brands, as in guitars. When we got ready to depart the plane, he handed me his card, inviting me to call if I ever needed anything.

Well, a light went on in my head, and I said, "As a matter of fact, we're shooting a video for a song called 'Burn Down The Trailer Park,' and I need a left-handed electric guitar for Billy Ray to use in the video." He told me he had just the guitar in mind and to come by the custom shop Monday.

When I showed up at Gibson, there was a guitar case sitting there at reception with a stickie note that read: *For Billy Ray Cyrus via Paul Abraham*. I opened the case and staring back at me was a brand new left-handed Gibson Les Paul Gold Top guitar. Wow! I knew that guitar would look great in the video, and it did. The following day, I drove over to Gibson to return the guitar, where I was informed that they didn't want it back. Henry had instructed the custom shop manager that the guitar was meant for Billy Ray and that he could just keep it. What? Billy Ray doesn't even play an electric guitar. I kept my mouth shut and took the guitar to Billy

Ray at the farm. He was equally flabbergasted. I sure wish I had a right-handed Gold Top! Henry? You hear that?

PART SIX

MORE LEGENDS

In Good Company

My absolute favorite rock-and-roll band on the planet back in the day was Free, with Paul Rodgers and Simon Kirke. Rock-and-roll's signature voice and the most rock-steady drummer around. I never dreamed that one day, I would become friends with those two legends. The band split and formed a new band called Bad Company—with Mick Ralphs from Mott the Hoople, Boz Burrell from King Crimson, Paul, and Simon— and hit the studio and released *Bad Co* in 1974. Many years later, Bad Company, with a new configuration, opened a couple of legs with Bad Company with Robert Hart singing, Simon on drums, Mick Ralphs on guitar, Dave "Bucket" Colwell on guitar, and Rick Wills (Foreigner) on bass. The band was fantastic, but the guys themselves were even better. I spent many an hour talking with Simon and the others.

The year was 1995, and Bad Co had planned some studio time in Nashville. Knowing that I lived nearby, they asked me if I could drive them from the studio to the hotel, and have an occasional night on the town. "We will pay you well." Charlie Brusco and Joe Boyland, their co-managers, and my friends were very happy for me to do this for them and so was I. Me . . . hanging out with a legendary band like Bad Company and getting paid for it. How in the world did I fall upon this dream job?

Our first night together, we went to the Ryman Auditorium— now, keep in mind, there were five of us crammed into my Silverado.

So, we pulled up in the alley behind the Ryman, I walked in and told the venue manager that I was with Bad Company, and they would like to have a short tour of the venue.

He said, "Absolutely," and we were given a guided tour of the Ole Opry. Porter and Ernest's dressing rooms, the stage, the seating, and the acoustics— all amazing. The history oozed out of the walls.

The manager asked me what plans the band had for the night. Our plans weren't much to speak of—a meal and then back to the hotel. The manager suggested we stop by to see the show: Junior Brown was opening for Allison Krause and Union Station.

Simon said: "We absolutely want to stay for that," and what Simon says . . . well, you know.

We went across the alley to Tootsie's and had dinner, and they had a few drinks and were feeling right. When we went back across the alley, we went through the back door of the Ryman and were met by Allison Krause, who had heard Bad Company was around and was one of her favorite bands. Well, how 'bout that?

We all enjoyed Allison's music and her sweet voice that night. Junior Brown was off-the-charts good too.

As we were getting ready to leave, Allison shows back up and asked us to meet her at Tootsie's to see a friend of hers playing some music. We got a table toward the back and really had a fabulous evening. Bekka Bramlett wandered in, and it was on, big time. She is a wild woman like her mama and can sing just like Bonnie. Before we left that night, we had two local artists who expressed an interest in adding some backup vocals on the new Bad Company album. Things were lining up. Before it was finished, Bad Co's friends who had helped on the album looked like this:

Joe Leo, acoustic guitar, production

Vince Gill, electric guitar

Dean Howard and Richie Sambora, guitars

Alison Krauss, fiddle, backing vocal

Matt Rollings, piano

Jim Capaldi, percussions

Bekka Bramlett, Kim Carnes, and Timothy B. Schmidt, backing vocals

The project was called *Stories Told and Untold*, and the album was released in 1996, though, regardless of the enormous talent, received very little critical acclaim and sales were flat.

———

A tour or two later, Paul Rodgers opened for Skynyrd, and I got to know him pretty well. During a downtime with Skynyrd, I was approached by Paul's manager about going out with Paul for some shows in Alabama and Mississippi. I obviously jumped at the opportunity. I mean, that man was the epitome of what a rock-and-roll voice should sound like, and songs like "Rock and Roll Fantasy" and "Can't Get Enough" and "All Right Now" could only be done real justice by the man who had sung the original notes. Howard Leese was his lead guitar player during this time, formerly the guitarist for Heart, and he was so much fun to be around.

———

Small World

While I was working for Michael Peterson, we were booked to play a nightclub on the Lower Eastside of Manhattan. After one of Skynyrd's buses took the mirror off of a Mercedes in Manhattan, I decided to leave all buses in Secaucus, New Jersey.

We crossed the East River via the tunnel on a commuter bus, and it dropped us off at the Port Authority, at which point the band and I took the subway to the street where the club was. We all jumped on the escalator and headed for street level, and when the escalator deposited us on the street, I almost walked right into Simon Kirke, Bad Co's drummer.

He and I both were so shocked we had to take a second look. It had been a couple of years since I'd worked with him in Nashville, but there was no mistaking either of us. We hugged each other and marveled at how on earth could this happen in Manhattan. The other guys with me were dumbfounded too. It is, without a doubt, a small world.

BRET MICHAELS

During one of our breaks, Billy Powell was asked to play on Poison's album, and he became close friends with Bret Michaels, the leader of the band. Bret came out to see Skynyrd on several occasions, and he and I became friends. While we were playing at the Woodlands in Houston, Texas, I walked in the dressing room to find Bret giving himself a shot and found out that he was diabetic. At first, I thought he may be shooting up some kind of drug, but it was only insulin.

A few years later, I was in Nashville running errands on Music Row, and as I'm turning onto one of the side streets, I hear someone say, "Hey, Paul," which was very surprising to me that anyone would recognize me on the streets of Music Row. What was even more surprising was that it was Bret Michaels. I guess I had made an impression on him.

We talked for a little while, and I informed him that I was now working for Billy Ray Cyrus. He gave me his phone number in California and asked me to stay in touch. At that time, Billy Ray was filming the show *Doc*, and the producers hooked up with a NASCAR team to put the show's logo and an image of Billy Ray Cyrus on the hood of the car. Coincidentally, the same team had featured Bret Michaels's solo project on the car earlier.

We were invited to a suite at a hotel in Dover, Delaware, the night before the race. A few weeks earlier, I had met the team owner and given him a copy of the *Drivin' Sideways* CD. In Dover, he told me how much he liked the CD and loved the fact that it was all racing-themed songs. There was another man in the room, and he asked what we were talking about. I told him about the project, and he asked me if I could send him a couple of copies to his office in Detroit, which I did the following Monday morning. He called me a few days later; he thought it was golden and said he had friends at one of the major auto manufacturers in Detroit that he wanted to pitch it to. He called me a day or two later to tell me that Ford was interested in purchasing a million copies to put in new vehicles. It made a lot of sense to me, so I was all in.

Well, this went on for a few weeks, and I started to get a little wary about this guy, and I remembered that Bret had met the same folks, so I called him. He told me the guy had told him the same exact thing and that it went on for a few weeks. I was advised to basically run like hell, because they guy was a fraud.

I remember exactly where I was when I called this guy and told him to buzz off. I was with Billy Ray Cyrus and Sly Dog, preparing to play at Richard Childress Racing's Christmas party.

My hopes had gotten so high from this guy because I knew the music was there and the market was there, so it made perfect sense what he was proposing. I'm not sure what makes people like him tick, but karma will bite him on the butt one of these days, that's for sure. Probably already has.

WAYLON AND JESSI

Circa 2001

I t was a fairly uneventful show day in Phoenix. We had come to town a day earlier and found out the Arizona Diamondbacks were playing the Atlanta Braves that night. Since most of the guys were Braves fans, it was a no-brainer. We'd found something to do. We entertained the fans around us with our best Billy Paul imitation of "Chipper, Chipper Jones . . . we have a thing going on." Of course, they got a kick out of us, but not nearly as much a kick as *we* got out of us.

Anyway, back to show day: not a lot going on. We didn't know a lot of folks from Phoenix, so we didn't have a huge guest list. We played cornhole in the parking lot and hung out on the bus. Billy Ray was flying in from California a few minutes before meet-and-greet. About the time he showed up, there was a commotion at the other end of the hall. I looked up to see Waylon Jennings and his lovely wife, Jessi Coulter, heading our way.

I said, "Billy Ray, look who's here."

We were all blown away and terribly starstruck. Waylon was moving slow, as he had been going through some health issues, but he was loud and cheerfully taunting Billy Ray with his good ole Southern-boy antics. They had a great visit, and later, Waylon and Jessi would join Billy Ray on stage for some "Good Hearted Woman." It was an awesome night for all of us, considering the day had started out so dull. Not long after that night, we learned that Waylon had passed away and left a huge hole in the Highwaymen. God bless him. As I am writing this, I just read that Jessi has just finished her book, *An Outlaw and a Lady*. I can't wait to read that one.

WILD BILL

My lifelong friend, Billy Clower, became an attorney in Mississippi after he attended Ole Miss and began his practice in our hometown of Leland, Mississippi. He was a character and a half. I know of no one who could be called an enemy of this guy. My first memory of him was in kindergarten when he fell off the sliding board and broke his arm. He blamed me for it in a joking kind of way. I'm not sure exactly how it happened, but I won't deny it. I guess I had a little bit of a mean streak.

While I was living in Colorado, Wild Bill, as he is known worldwide, came for a visit. Little did I know, he had pulled up stakes in Mississippi and was looking to resettle in Colorado. This was about the time a certain person back in Mississippi persuaded me to move back and go in with him to build a nightclub in Tupelo.

So I was leaving Colorado, and Bill was staying. Later, I would learn that Wild Bill had become a ski bum at Copper Mountain and would never return to Mississippi. I, on the other hand, though in love with the state of Colorado, find myself back in the heat and mosquitoes of the South to this day.

Some years later, we reconnected, and Gloria Reed Virden and I, along with Ronnie and Linda Petro Raney, went to visit Wild Bill in Leadville, Colorado, where he owned the Leadville Hostel. This place was fabulous. He had room to accommodate dozens of people. He gave us a room that was big enough for ten people, and we stayed there for a solid week. Bill's wife Cathy was less enthusiastic about us, but she grew to love us eventually. We skied, snowmobiled, and did a lot of sightseeing during our time there. As it turned out, our only cost was for the roundtrip airfare and a rental car, and whatever food we decided to have. It was an incredible week with Wild Bill and Cathy, and of course, Crazy Howard, Bill's brother.

The next time I got back out there was a couple of years later. It was in the fall during the elk rut. We rode four-wheelers all over those mountains around Leadville. We used logging and mining trails and navigated our way through some breathtaking scenery, and finally stood on the top of Mosquito Pass to take in the 360-degree view. Crazy Howard and Wild Bill, two of Leland's favorite sons, pretty much taking over the town of Leadville.

Two years after that, I got a message on my voicemail from Crazy Howard. "Paul, call me back, and I'll tell you what happened." Ominous words.

I called him back and learned that Bill's car left the road and hit a tree. He'd passed away at a Denver hospital. Those words stung me deeply. My oldest friend in the world, gone. I couldn't believe that a man so full of life was dead. I hooked up with a friend, Mike Long, and we drove out for Bill's memorial service at the hostel. Terry Morrison and John Wayne Vineyard also drove out. There were a lot of folks there to celebrate his life. We rode up on the mountain and picked up a big rock, took it back down, and had everybody there sign it, then we returned it to where we found it. His ashes were later spread in the Rocky Mountains that he so loved. He will often be remembered by the many people he touched.

Wild Bill Clower looking over the Rockies that he loved so much.

THE ALLMAN BROTHERS

Gregg Allman passed away during the writing of this book. His music always meant so much to me. The very first time I heard the Allman Brothers was on a stereo system with two Bose 901 speakers. We were at a friend's house way out in the country, east of Atlanta, and "Statesboro Blues" came on. I was blown away, not only by the Bose speakers, but by this phenomenal band. *Who is that?* My buddy informed me then of the Allman Brothers, Gregg and Duane, and their band, out of Macon, Georgia.

Well, needless to say, the Allman Brothers impacted us all, and especially Ronnie Van Zant, who considered Duane Allman his musical hero. Ronnie would preface his rock anthem, "Free Bird," with a dedication to Duane every night. Contrary to popular belief, there was never a rift or a competition between the two bands. Although both were considered Southern Rock bands, they were markedly different in styles. The Allman Brothers had a jazzy, bluesy style, and Skynyrd had a hard rocking/slightly country, kick-you-in-the-ass style. Both bands, to me, were at the top of their games when adversity struck, and although they'd made music through it all, so much was lost from the original bands that my listening habits usually are pretty dated. For me, the Beatles, the Allman Brothers, and the original Skynyrd are the top of the heap forever and laid the groundwork for the others to follow. Good luck filling those shoes.

THE DOOBIE BROTHERS

The Doobie Brothers were some great guys to hang out with when they opened for Skynyrd on a tour. I always loved their music and was ecstatic when I heard they were going to be on tour with us. We gave Tom Johnston a ride on Skynyrd's bus from the San Francisco airport to the venue, and it was probably too far for him. I'm sure he thought he was back in the '70s again. Patrick Simmons and John McFee were both very quiet, but incredible guitar players, and Patrick did a lot of vocals too.

My favorite Doobie was Keith Knudsen, who was married to a girl from Jackson, Mississippi. He and I had fun talking about the Mississippi Rain and Sassy Jones days, two bands that my friends Johnny Crocker and George Allen played in. Sadly, Keith is gone, but certainly not forgotten. Michael Hassock was really the most outgoing of all of them. He, too, has passed. I can still hear the Doobies music ringing out in the night air. What a great band and bunch of guys.

MISSISSIPPI'S FAVORITE SONS

Gone, too, is my old friend mentioned above, George "All Night" Allen, a Mississippi Delta staple, and one of the best bass players around. He was born into a family of musicians and fun-loving folks, and it's been told they could go all night, picking and singing in their living room. George played with everybody. A lot of the blues guys loved to get George to play because he could follow their unorthodox style of picking. Anybody who knows any real bluesmen—singing the old rawbone blues styles—knows they may not have the best meter in the world and it takes a helluva bass player to keep up with it.

George and Johnny Crocker came to Atlanta while I was living there and had planned to try their hand down in Macon, Georgia, where the Allman Brothers were just exploding. Little Jimmy Henderson was with them, and he went on to play with Black Oak Arkansas. I think we partied so much they never made it to Macon, and if they did, I never knew what came of it.

Jimmy was a Jackson boy, and he was a virtuoso on electric guitar. Jimmy, too, has passed on.

George died in a one-vehicle accident on the Old Leland Road just past the cemetery, and his sister, Liz Anne, makes sure there is always something there to remember her brother—a cross with one of George's bandanas keeps him in a lot of Delta folks' memories when they travel that road, as I often do. Johnny

Crocker, I'm happy to say is still making music in the Jackson, Mississippi, area.

Greenville, Mississippi, is the hometown of Bud Cockrell, who went on to play with Pablo Cruise, It's a Beautiful Day, and Cockrell and Santos. Bud passed away in 2010 and is buried near his hometown.

Another very talented musician and songwriter who also claims Greenville as his hometown is Bruce Blackman. He was the driving force of the band, Starbuck, and the band's single "Moonlight Feels Right" is still played regularly on many radio stations around the country. Bruce was in the Greenville band Eternity's Children, along with Starbuck's Bo Wagner and Greenville legend Johnny Walker. Johnny and Bo have passed away, and Bruce is still making music near Atlanta—and from what he tells me, he, too, is writing a book.

Through the years, I have lost many musician friends, and I'm certain about one thing . . . the jams that are going on in Heaven are "Hellacious."

The Moody Blues

When we booked Skynyrd in 1974, our responsible agent was Terry Rhodes of the Paragon Agency in Macon, Georgia. Years later, when I actually was working for Skynyrd and living in Colorado, I learned that Terry was the responsible agent for my second most favorite band of all times behind the Beatles—the Moody Blues.

I found out that the Moody Blues were going to be at Red Rocks Amphitheatre, along with the Colorado Symphony, and the performances would be filmed for a special video of the event. I jumped at the news and fired off an email to Terry. Luckily, he remembered me and set me up with three tickets to see the show from about twelve rows from the stage.

My wife and I, accompanied by our friend, Barb Robinson, made the trek from the parking lot up the hill to the Will Call window. In this business, it's a crapshoot sometimes as to whether the comped tickets would be there, and if they weren't, it would be a long trip down off the mountain and back home. Terry came through for us with flying colors.

The show opened with an overture by the Symphony, using excerpts from some of their more famous songs in the orchestral deliverance. It was moving to say the very least, but when Graeme Edge took center stage and began his recitation, "Breathe deep the gathering gloom . . ." well, I lost it. I got this huge lump in my throat, and it stayed there the entire show. I was literally on the verge of tears the entire time. And the smile on my face hurt after a while, but it stayed right there.

As the show progressed, the full moon in the eastern sky over Denver lifted over the rock formation that housed the stage, giving the show a special effect delivered by God. Other than the Beatles show in Memphis ages ago, this was as close as I have ever come to a religious experience at a concert.

I saw the Moodys one other time when I lived in Atlanta, and from that day on, I owned everything they ever put out. Their music and lyrics inspired me through the years to try to be a better person. I'm sure I failed in that effort a lot of times, but the music still moves me all the same.

PART SEVEN

I, PAUL ABRAHAM

ROUNDABOUT AND BACK AGAIN

Nowadays, I still live in the Mississippi Delta in a quiet little village called Scott. For many years, this town thrived as the headquarters of Delta and Pine Land. D&PL sold out many years ago to Monsanto, and now Monsanto has sold out to Bayer. It's changed drastically over the years, but it's still a sleepy little town, and that's just how I like it.

The meeting place in town is the Scott Store, open for breakfast and lunch, Monday through Friday. The food is excellent, and the company is even better. Charles and Shirley Shamoun are the proprietors, and if you ever need to know what goes on in Scott, that's the place to go.

We also have a fine restaurant here in Scott called 5 O'Clock on Deer Creek, or Bubba's, for short. Bubba Roden is one of those characters who, once you meet him, you will never forget him. The restaurant doesn't exactly exude ambience, or at least the kind that some of the snootier Delta folks like. Bubba's is usually full of farmers and hunters and a bunch of good ole boys and good ole girls.

He has live music on some nights, and when he first opened, I would go in, and Raymond Longoria, a Mississippi Delta country singer, would ask me to play while he took a dinner break. I've always had a bad case of stage fright, and I guess that's why none of the musicians I worked with knew I played and sang.

When Raymond played there, Eden Brent, the Delta's favorite

blues artist, and her family would come out to hear him play, and they always loved it when I got up. They had a table full of folks, and it was so loud in there, I could hardly hear myself think. I started out with "Paradise" by John Prine, or "Muhlenberg County" as it may be better known, and the noise actually subsided, and folks were listening. People were still coming in and the tables were full.

There was another night when Eden's father, Howard Brent, told me that Julia Reed was coming with a special guest, and they would be sitting at their table. In a few minutes, Julia came in the door with much fanfare, and had Jessica Lange right behind her. Oh my God. I wasn't sure if I could sing another song with my stage fright getting worse, and now Jessica Lange was sitting fifteen feet from where I was attempting to entertain.

I did another Prine song called "Far From Me," and she did acknowledge my efforts with applause and a nod of her head.

Bubba always came up and helped me sing "Me and Paul" by Willie Nelson. By the time he had fed all the folks that had come in, he had pretty much consumed a fifth of Patron and was walking around the room giving people shots. He was prone to dance on the tables, and he never failed to entertain all of us. I'm proud to say Bubba and Linda Roden are friends and neighbors here in Scott.

THE KIDS

One big regret I have to endure in my life is the fact that I never had children of my own. Sandie had a beautiful little girl, and I was her father from age three on. She blessed us with three grandkids, Derek, Samantha, and Alexis, whom I loved as if they were my own, and they all loved me back.

Kids have always had a special place in my heart, and that is one thing I would have done differently if I had it to do all over again. I always used the excuse that I didn't want to bring children into this crazy world, and although the world has only gotten worse, I do regret it. My grandkids grew up, and sadly, we grew apart. I never get to see them anymore, and the fact that Samantha has two kids that I have never seen really stings. It's nobody's fault but my own.

Later on in life, after Sandie and I were divorced, I met and started dating Gloria Virden, or Gloria Reed, as I knew her in high school. We met at my brother Carl's memorial service and started seeing each other shortly after that. Carl and Gloria were inseparable through the years. Carl would always talk to me about Gloria, and he was her self-proclaimed guardian. During Christmas 2009, I traveled to Memphis where Gloria lived and worked as a hair stylist at Kirby Pines, an exceptional retirement community. She was at Ronnie and Linda Raney's house, decorating for Christmas.

That very day, I talked them into taking a trip to Colorado to go skiing with Wild Bill Clower, and I booked flights, a rental car, and talked to Bill about staying at his hostel in Leadville. In three weeks, we were on our way, and man, did we have a ball. Gloria and I got along really well and we started dating at that point. A few weeks later, we all went to see Jersey Boys at the Orpheum Theatre in Memphis, and shortly after that, I moved in with Gloria.

From time to time, her daughter, Katie, and son-in-law, Jeff, would come to Memphis to visit, and they would bring their two boys, Jackson and Joe. I became attached to those two right away. A year or so later, Katie became pregnant with twins, and there were horrible complications, concerning a missing chromosome in both twins. Gloria decided she needed to be back in the Mississippi Delta to help Katie with her pregnancy and the boys, since Katie was having to spend days on end with her doctors, so we moved to Cleveland. As it turned out, one of the twins passed away at birth, and the doctors told them there was a good chance that the surviving twin would be terribly deformed and would potentially have problems her entire life.

I practically raised that sweet child myself, teaching her how to hold her bottle and helping her with her speaking and learning. I am so happy to say that other than being a little smaller than kids of her age, she is absolutely perfect. And oh yeah . . . she loves me! Even today, when asked whom she wants to sit by at the dinner table, it's always "Pauly." It's a bit embarrassing for me because she chooses me over her grandparents, parents, and anyone else in the room. There is no doubt I would do anything in the world for this sweet angel.

I now am helping Katie with her new business called Open Season. Katie is a fabulous artist, and we have begun putting her artwork on t-shirts, pillows, and prints. We have done fairly well in this highly competitive business and have fifty-plus stores in six states carrying the line.

For the readers who would like to see what we are doing, you can go to www.openseasonppt.com.

GUS JOHNSON

When my father had an office on Poplar Street in Greenville, I worked for him, calling on accounts and typing the daily logs. I would go to lunch right down the street at Jim's Cafe, an old-timey cafe, where all the locals would meet for breakfast and lunch. It wasn't just the food that gave me nourishment. The owner, Gus Johnson, would always come sit down with me and talk to me about any subject that might arise.

He was a wonderful friend to me in those days, and even after I showed a great failure in judgment in my personal life, his friendship never faltered. Gus genuinely cared for me, as he did everyone he came in contact with. He loved to hunt and fish, and ride his bicycle, but most of all, he loved to tell stories. So many people would come in to hear his stories or to share their stories with him. The food was great but was always secondary to me. I just loved talking to Gus. He would tell so many stories about himself and his best friend, Joe Virden, whom I have become well acquainted with in the past few years.

When I moved back to the Delta after being away for thirty years, I made a beeline to Jim's Cafe to visit with Gus. Nothing had changed in the cafe. Every picture that had been on his Wall of Fame back then was still there, although a little yellower from age.

Gus had aged very well, and he remembered me instantly. We sat and talked for what seemed like hours, between Gus's trips to the cash register. He told me he had kept up with me through some mutual friends and that he wanted to hear all about my travels. Well, it seems that every time I went in, Gus was so busy, I never really got the chance to talk about all that had transpired with me in the past thirty years. Then came the word from his daughter Evelyn that Gus was in the ICU in Jackson, and he was not doing well at all. In true Gus Johnson form, he recuperated nicely, but it was evident to me his illness had taken a toll on him. He was still at the cafe regularly for a year or so, and then he quit coming up there.

Evelyn had felt that Gus may not have too much longer left in the world, so she contacted all of his old friends for a get-together with Gus at the cafe. When Gloria and I got there, it was almost completely full of people I had not seen in years, and they were all there for their friend, Gus Johnson. We visited and had some pictures made with Gus, and it was a wonderful event to be a part of.

It wasn't too terribly long after that when we got the word Gus had passed away quietly with his family all around him, just the way he would have wanted it. His funeral at the Catholic Church completely filled every pew, and people were standing all around the congregation against the walls. Gus was given a posthumous commendation from the city, and all in attendance celebrated his life. He was truly one of a kind, and a great friend.

DEER CREEK

eer Creek begins its flow through the Delta a quarter mile down the street at Lake Bolivar. Deer Creek has been a part of my life, practically from day one. The creek flows in front of our house, and our driveway is actually a bridge across the creek. It meanders through Leland, and the town has always made it a beautiful scene. There are cypress trees, magnolia trees, crepe myrtles, and many other types of trees, bushes, and flowers lining the creek. At Christmastime, the townspeople build and decorate floats with various Christmas scenes, and it becomes a large event for the entire season.

Deer Creek has a storied past too. The tale is told of General Grant taking his gunships down Deer Creek to the Yazoo River and on into Vicksburg, where the Siege of Vicksburg had already begun. Legend has it that at least one of his boats was sunk in Deer Creek, and muskets and musket balls can still be found in or near the creek after all these years.

The creek bank had two special meanings at Leland High School—one, it was where people went to smoke their cigarettes, and the other, if someone had a disagreement in school, it was always followed by, "Meet me on the creek bank after school." And the fight would be on.

I'm not sure why we all liked to fight so much back in the day. There were Friday nights when Robert McClellan and I would go out, just knowing we were going to get into a scrap with someone that night. I'm not sure if it was a Delta thing, but it sure happened an awful lot. I had a terrible reputation as a fighter, and it took laying off the beer and smoking a little weed instead to ease up that mean streak. I was just a big old teddy bear after that.

THE MUSIC IN ME

I still play music almost daily. Most of the time, I play by myself and for myself. A few years ago, we were having a class reunion for our entire school. My cousin Dianne was spearheading the event and asked me, "Didn't you have a band in high school?"

Well, the next thing I knew . . .

Harry "Bub" Branton and Johnny Keen, two good friends I had played some with back then, were rehearsing to play for the reunion. We picked up Ralph Morrow on bass, and Hal Holbrook on drums. We called our band That'll Do, because after we rehearsed a song, we would invariably say, "That'll Do!"

Our first night together, we realized it was going to be easy to pull this off. We came up with a set list and played for a solid three hours and didn't even finish the list. Mostly songs from the '50s and '60s . . . with a few from the '70s thrown in.

Since then, we have played at several events, festivals, and local restaurants, but our favorite gig is playing at Magnolia Gardens, an assisted living facility in Greenville. Jo Ann Fava has become a fan of our band, and she is the administrator of the home, so we play there about once a month.

Some of the people I have known all my life are residents there.

Sam Cefalu, the father of three of my best friends, Phil, Claire, and Joann, lives there, and even at ninety-six years old, he still wants to dance to every song.

B.C. Lundy is also there. His kids were my friends growing up.

Junior Carollo resides there, and his daughters, Terry and Patsy, were good friends of mine.

Virginia Hart Virden's mother and father are both there.

Darla Branton's (Bub's wife) one hundred-year-old mother is there as well.

They all enjoy us Leland guys coming to entertain them from time to time, and it is sure a pleasure for us to do it.

That's a Wrap

People often tell me I have had such an interesting life, and I certainly have to agree, although a little less excitement would have been okay with me. I know that once this book is published, there will be many more stories that come to my mind, so maybe a Volume Two is not out of the question.

I plan to continue living my life the way I always have, but my travels will be limited to few and far between. I know that one day I will live in Colorado again, and if I have my choice, Freddie Ravner will be my neighbor again. There is something to be admired about the life he leads in the Rockies, living at the end of a dead-end road on ten beautiful acres with God's footprints all around him. I want that again. As long as I can have a dog or two to keep me warm at night, not much else matters.

I will continue to play my guitar and sing, if only for myself and my dogs. I will always love children and try to show them the right paths to take in life—and I certainly know the paths not to take, because I took every one of them. I will continue to listen to my elders, even though I have entered that classification myself and, regretfully, most of my elders have passed on. So, all you young'uns, consider me your elder, and don't do what I did.

I found out early in life that a nine-to-five just didn't suit me, although I did it for a long time. Being on the road with a rock-and-roll or country band, for that matter, was pretty dang cool and a load of fun, but they don't give out pensions in the music business, or at least on my side of it. You kids: go to school, get a degree or a vocation, work hard every day, and put your money away. Feel free to buy all the concert tickets or CDs you want, but don't buy into what some roadies will try to sell. It's hard work, morning, noon, and night. Certainly not for the weak of heart.

It's not always the best situation for a marriage either. It was hard to leave my wife at home in the mountains and traipse all over the world, to feel helpless when she called about some problem at home. Sandie was a brave woman and that lifestyle suited her better than any other she could have had. She made a lot of sacrifices to make sure I got to do the music-business gig, and I will always be in her debt. She will say that our time together in Colorado was the best time of her life, and I concur. It was magical, and is missed.

As I finish these chronicles of my life, I am proud to say that the words of my friend, Ronnie Van Zant, in "Simple Man," have steered my way of thinking about life. The songs Ronnie wrote are masterpieces, in my humble opinion, and they are timeless and ageless. Let the music live on forever.

Thanks to all who took the time to read my stories, and especially, thanks to the people whom the stories are about. Without you all, my life would have been terribly dull.

—Paul Abraham
The Gospel According to Abraham

Photo Credit: John Keen Photography

CPSIA information can be obtained
at www.ICGtesting.com
Printed in the USA
BVHW042025141219
566651BV00005B/10/P